CALM IN THE MOUNTAIN STORM

CALL OF THE ROCKIES ~ BOOK 9

MISTY M. BELLER

Misty M. Beller
BOOKS

ISBN-13 Trade Paperback: 978-1-954810-54-9

ISBN-13 Large Print Paperback: 978-1-954810-55-6

ISBN-13 Casebound Hardback: 978-1-954810-56-3

How precious also are thy thoughts unto me, O God!
How great is the sum of them!
If I should count them, they are more in number than the sand:
when I awake, I am still with thee.

Psalm 139:17-18 (KJV)

CHAPTER 1

A warning bell clanged through Elise Turner's body. Something didn't feel right.

The winter wind swept through the valley, and she pulled her buffalo coat tighter, straining to make out details of the lodges ahead. Were she and her companions too far away to hear sounds of the children who normally played on the land near the camp? Perhaps. But she should be able to see figures moving among the dwellings now.

She looked at her brother astride his gelding. "Does something seem off to you?"

They rode at least a minute farther as Ben studied the Salish village. A glance behind showed their friends, White Owl and Lola, also staring at their destination.

"It does seem quiet." Though Ben's voice held its usual measured tone, his words sped up the thud of her heartbeat.

"Do you think visitors have come? Is that why everything is

so still?" Lola spoke just loudly enough for them all to hear, then her voice softened as she murmured something to her husband.

Lola reached from her horse to White Owl's and took their tiny babe from his arms, and the child's little fussing sounds drifted forward. Elise's heart squeezed. Baby Anna was only two months old now—or two moons, as the natives said it. Either way, she was the perfect age to cuddle. White Owl had kept the cradleboard secured to his chest during most of their day's ride, but he must have handed their daughter off to his wife in case he needed to protect them from possible danger ahead.

White Owl participated so much in the babe's care. Who would imagine that a Shoshone brave would change soiled diapers as often as his wife did? The white fathers Elise knew rarely did such a thing. Her own pa had been present with his children more than many men in their community, taking one or two at a time along when he visited the sick or ailing as the reverend of their parish. But he'd left care of the babes to Mama and the rest of the girls. Seeing White Owl sweetly cradle little Anna always brought an ache to Elise's chest.

As Lola slipped her arms through the straps on the cradle board, White Owl rode up on Ben's other side. His voice dropped so low, Elise had to strain to make out his words, still thick with his Shoshone accent. "There is the smell of death ahead. The hungry birds circle."

Even as his words sent a shiver down her back, her gaze flicked to the sky above the camp. She'd not been mistaken about those turkey vultures. Had the entire village left camp to attend a burial?

Tightness clogged her throat. There had been enough death already. A funeral was the very reason the four of them had gone down to the Nez Perce village a day's ride to the south. A messenger had come to say Narrow Feet had passed away. Dear Narrow Feet, the first man of his people who'd finally opened his heart to the miracle of God's love and grace. In every village where they stopped to share the gospel, the people there would be resistant until a single person finally softened. Then one by one, others would come to meet the Lord for themselves. In that Nez Perce camp, Narrow Feet had been the one who turned the tide, the start of a harvest of souls greater than they'd seen in any other camp where they'd preached. Narrow Feet himself had shared about God's love nearly as much as she and Ben.

And now the Lord had taken him to paradise. A wonderful example of the hope for every believer, but the grief on earth was impossible to ignore.

In this Salish town where they were now returning, there hadn't yet been that one person to step forward and accept God's grace. Yet perhaps something they'd said had planted a seed, and the harvest had been reaped in their absence.

Lord, let that be the case. Only You can bring forth the yield of souls. Open their hearts to Your love.

It was the prayer she'd been praying since arriving at the first Shoshone village she and Ben had worked in a year and a half ago. The place where they'd met White Owl and been blessed to watch his faith spring to life. He hadn't joined them in their work back then, though they'd invited him to come with them as interpreter. He and Lola had found them later in the Nez Perce village of Narrow Feet, and they'd been so much help since then—a blessing in too many ways to number. White Owl's skills as an interpreter were invaluable, and Lola's presence as a white woman who'd married into one of the tribes carried a great deal of reassurance for the people.

And little Anna. Having her around doubled the joy in every day. Elise had assisted her own mother in raising her own seven younger siblings—there were twelve of them in their family—so one might think she'd be tired of little ones. But they were such a joy, especially while the babes were young enough to be cute and hadn't yet acquired a mischievous streak.

"Elise, you and Lola stay here while White Owl and I ride

ahead to see what's happened." Ben's voice held that tone of command he used when he was trying to keep her from running into what he considered danger. He was one of those youngsters she'd helped raise, but he'd always considered himself her protector, even as a boy.

They weren't riding into danger though. This would likely be grief.

He'd turned his focus to her, brows raised as he waited for her answer.

"All right." She could let the two men go on ahead. She and Lola would follow a little behind.

As they nudged their horses into a trot, she slowed her mare enough for Lola to ride up alongside.

"I don't like the looks of this." Her friend's voice came out in a hushed singsong as she stroked the soft black hair atop Anna's head. "The place looks deserted."

Maybe the entire camp had needed to move on suddenly. Yet wouldn't they have taken the lodges?

White Owl and Ben had covered half the distance to the village, but they slowed their horses to walk, studying whatever they saw.

Elise nudged her mount into a trot. "I'm going to catch up with them."

"Wait. Elise, no." Lola's words faded in the breeze, and Elise sent a look of apology over her shoulder for ignoring her friend's concerns. She didn't want Lola to be displeased with her, but she had to know what had happened.

She turned her focus back to the camp, but nothing changed in its appearance. Not until she reached just past the place the men had slowed.

Was that someone lying on the ground? She reined her mare to a walk and studied the figure. The pressure tightening her chest plunged into her belly, weighting her insides like a mill-stone. The main path between the lodges was not a safe spot for someone to lie. The striped fur wrapped around the figure looked like the one Crying Wolf usually wore. If she'd fallen and injured herself, why would the others leave her, even if they'd been forced to abandon the camp in haste?

Then her gaze caught another form, and her throat closed. A sob wrenched through her chest. That little body. Could that be Runs Like the Wind lying prone at the base of his lodge? Then the bright red mark on his buckskin tunic glared at her. She clutched the base of her neck and tore her gaze away.

Lord, what happened here? Not the child. Not Runs Like the Wind.

She'd stroked the loose hair from his face only last week as he looked up at her and pronounced his name in English. His dark eyes had sparkled with pleasure. Though many adults in this camp still eyed her and Ben and Lola and White Owl with distrust, the children had let the missionaries into their lives and hearts quickly.

Would she never see that sweet smile again?

Ben and White Owl had paused at the edge of the village, and she let her gaze move toward them, doing her best to block out Crying Wolf's body, which lay just beyond their horses.

White Owl dismounted and stepped toward the form, his stride hesitant. He'd likely seen his share of death growing up and training as a Shoshone warrior. Thank the Lord, he now spoke out for peace...God's peace.

White Owl stepped past Crying Wolf's body, then lifted the flap of the lodge behind her and peered inside. He turned back and spoke to Ben, too quietly for her to make out his words. Her brother slipped from his horse's back and moved into the village, heading down a different row of huts.

She halted her mare behind the men's horses, keeping the animals as a buffer to block out the sight of the two fallen bodies. Her entire body ached with their loss. Had Runs Like the Wind understood the stories Elise told of Creator Father who loved him so much He would give his most important possession for the boy? How much could a five-year-old comprehend through sign language and the few words Elise learned in his tongue?

The cry of a baby jerked her gaze up, and she glanced back at Lola. But her friend had halted her horse too far back for the sound to be from Anna. The mewling cry sounded like it came from a different direction.

Elise turned back to the camp. Maybe it had been an effect of the wind. She scanned the lodges, her gaze moving around and between them. But as her mind registered more lumps on the ground that looked too much like fallen people, her belly churned. Surely this couldn't be a massacre of the entire village. She'd not let her mind consider that possibility before, and she couldn't stand the thought now. She forced her gaze to the side, toward the thin strip of trees that shaded the river's edge.

A figure there made her breath catch. Her body tensed as she focused on him.

An Indian warrior, standing tall as he stared into the empty camp. He stood at least thirty strides away from her, but even from this distance, she could see the strength in the broad shoulders under his buckskin tunic.

Was he one of the attackers? Maybe he'd stayed behind to make sure none of their victims still lived. Or he might be simply taking a few extra minutes to pleasure in their victory.

She should scream. Alert Ben and White Owl.

But something about the way the brave stood gave her pause. He didn't puff out his chest or raise a bloody knife in triumph. As the wind brushed loose hair from his face, his outline spoke of grief. Maybe even loneliness.

He held something in his left arm. She focused on the spot. A blanket? It was gray with bright red accents.

An infant's cry sounded, the same tone as before, but louder.

Her heart hiccupped at the same moment the warrior looked down at the blanket in his arms. Had he taken a baby from the village before massacring the other inhabitants? Whose child did he have? Yet even as the question flitted through her mind, recognition flared. That was the blanket Bright Eyes had been so proud of using to wrap her new baby girl.

This warrior held Pretty Shield.

Elise started to scream, but the man's gaze lifted from the bundle in his arms and met hers. Even over the distance, the intensity of his eyes held her fixed. His expression spoke of desperation, not at all the defiant look of victory. Was there a chance he *wasn't* one of the killers?

Either way, she had to get Pretty Shield away from him—without letting the infant be hurt. The only chance to do that was to get the brave to willingly hand over the child.

She nudged her horse toward him, keeping the mare's gait slow. White Owl and Ben were nearby. If she screamed, they would be at her side in an instant. And she also had the rifle Ben insisted she keep strapped to her saddle when they rode. She would never use it on a person, but if she needed to, she could aim the gun in this man's direction and make him think she would shoot.

But first she needed to attempt a peaceable request. Surely he had no use for a baby.

Pretty Shield cried out again, and though the man didn't move his gaze from Lola, he lifted his arm in a gentle bounce, a motion that might soothe a fussy infant. As though he'd held a little one like this before.

"Elise, no!" Ben's voice barked through the air, making her nerves jump at the unexpected sound. Footsteps pounded the ground. Her brother must be running toward them.

The brave's attention jerked that direction, and his hand flew to a tomahawk strapped to his side. He slipped the weapon out and raised it before Elise could take in a breath to speak. The Indian began to back away, but he held that tomahawk poised to fling.

7

She spun toward her brother. "Ben, stop!"

Her yell didn't even slow him. The brave was backing away faster now, gripping little Pretty Shield tighter to his chest. The babe had begun crying in earnest. Was he squeezing too tight, or was the child hungry? Or maybe she sensed the horror that was about to happen here.

Elise had to stop this. Raising her voice to a shout, she infused her sharpest big-sister tone. "Ben, stop!"

He slowed, his stride moving from a sprint to a jog as he looked to her. She stretched her palm toward him. "He has a baby." Even if the Indian understood English, that shouldn't make him angry.

Ben slowed to a walk as he looked at the stranger, then he seemed to fully understand the situation, and he halted completely. "Who are you?" Her brother's voice was far rougher than usual. No doubt, he would be seeing the images of the dead he'd just witnessed for many days to come.

The man didn't answer. He'd already backed deeper into the trees, and he still held his tomahawk raised. But he looked like he might run instead of fighting. Did he have a horse nearby? She slid a look through the woods upriver but saw no sign of an animal.

Perhaps he would feel less cornered if she instead of her brother asked the questions. If the brave could even understand her words. She couldn't think of a single motion in the tribes' sign language that would speak what she needed to ask, so she'd have to use English.

She swallowed the lump in her throat and willed the pounding in her heart to slow as she raised her voice. "Who are you, and what are you doing with Bright Eyes's baby?"

*G*oes Ahead froze as he studied the white woman. How did she know his wife's name? And that this was her child? Who were these strangers who appeared the same day the entire village was murdered?

In his arms, Pretty Shield's cries grew louder, and he forced his hold to loosen. Perhaps he was gripping her too tight. Everything in him wanted to wrap both arms around his daughter and sprint far away from these people. But he couldn't react from fear. These white men had rifles and horses, and he had neither. He couldn't risk his own life or that of his tiny daughter.

He forced himself to stand his ground and meet the woman's gaze. Both his children needed him to live and fight for them. He was the only family they had left, and they were everything to him.

CHAPTER 2

"Who are you? How do you know my wife?" Goes Ahead studied the faces of the white people as he spoke, and he didn't miss the surprise that splashed across their features. Especially the woman who'd spoken Bright Eyes's name.

Sitting atop her horse, she looked small, but the flash in her gaze made it clear she wasn't the kind to stand by and hold in her thoughts.

Her eyes narrowed in the way that said she was trying to uncover a secret. "You are Bright Eyes's husband?" The woman's gaze dipped to the squirming, fussing bundle in his arms, and realization slipped through her expression. She was understanding he was also the father of this babe his wife had named Pretty Shield.

She honed her focus back on his face, and her eyes narrowed even more. "Where have you been? We've stayed with this tribe two mo—I mean *moons* now. I have not seen you."

Surely Bright Eyes would have told this curious woman if she'd asked. His wife had been so panicked over their son being taken by that Sioux war party, she wouldn't have hesitated to speak of it. Of course, Bright Eyes knew only a few words in the white man's tongue. He'd been teaching her a little, but not enough to speak well.

But the way this woman watched him... She must know where he'd been. Too much understanding shone in her eyes. So why would she test him? Perhaps to determine for certain if he was the babe's father?

Or maybe the white people had brought on this attack. These four weren't enough to have done the killing themselves, but their presence so soon after the murders here couldn't be an accident. They must have made a treaty with the Sioux dogs for this massacre.

Angry bile roiled in his belly as he fought to keep his gaze from moving to where his wife's still body lay twisted. He'd been moving Pretty Shield to a safe location under the trees before returning to care for Bright Eyes's lifeless form, but these white people had appeared before he could return to the place of death.

The stranger was still watching him, waiting for his answer. He could hold his tongue. In fact, he should be the one asking questions.

But it would hurt nothing to tell of his successful conquest to recapture his son. They, with their rifles and horses, should know he was a warrior, able to protect his children even without a gun and mount.

*H*e lifted his chin. "I have chased down the Sioux war party that took my son. I have won against my enemies."

Something like panic crossed the woman's face, and her gaze moved past him, searching. Did she fear he'd killed the entire Sioux party? He should have. Then they wouldn't have been able to ride ahead of him and exact their revenge on his village.

Fresh anger burned through him. He'd been focused on saving his son without putting the boy in more danger, so he'd stolen him away from the Sioux. He should have thought more about vengeance and killed them all. Then his wife and her people would not be dead. His throat ached so much he could barely breathe.

And this woman. If she feared for his enemies, that proved these white people were enemies too.

When she spoke again, her voice rose higher. "Your son. Did you not get him back? Is he hurt?"

That wasn't what he'd expected her to say. Was there a deeper reason the Sioux had taken only *his* child the first time they came? Perhaps to sell him to these white people? He'd thought Walking Bird was the only one stolen because he'd been the easiest to grab—playing by the river while Bright Eyes rested in the shade.

But this woman's words proved she knew of his boy.

"I have taken back my son. He is safe now. Where no one can find him." He would make sure that was true. He'd tucked Walking Bird away in the shelter of the rocks while he came to make sure all was well in the village. A good thing. Now he just had to get his daughter away from these people and make sure they didn't follow him.

Relief eased her features. "Good. Bright Eyes was certain you would bring him home." Her voice broke when she spoke his wife's name, and she turned to stare toward the place where her body lay. Even from this angle, he could see the way her eyes rimmed red. As though she grieved these deaths.

But that couldn't be so. These white people had caused the massacre.

In his arms, Pretty Shield let out a sharp cry, and the woman spun back to him. He jostled the babe to soothe her, but her squeals continued.

The woman slid from her horse and started toward him,

concern marking her features. Her gaze was on his daughter, as though she planned to reach out and take her.

He gripped Pretty Shield closer and raised his tomahawk again. "Stop."

"Elise!" the white man called to her. A heartbeat later, the click of a rifle told him what his eyes didn't have to confirm.

He could fling his ax and hit her easily, but a bullet would tear through him in the next moment. And his children needed him. He couldn't let these strangers have his daughter and son.

He held his pose but spoke instead of acting. "Come no closer."

Pretty Shield had quieted when he called out, but now she began wailing again.

The woman nodded toward her, then raised her voice to be heard over the babe. "I only meant to come and soothe her. I think she's hungry."

A new tightening pressed in his chest. He'd not considered how to feed his daughter. She needed milk. Could he find a mother deer or buffalo to provide enough for her? That would be a challenge with the cold months coming on. Most had already weaned their young.

And he would have to kill the animal to gather its milk. Which meant he'd need many such creatures along the way before he reached his father's tribe across the mountains. How could he manage that through the tallest peaks? The goats and curved-horn sheep, perhaps.

Desperation clenched his belly. He'd done the impossible before when he had to. Kept himself alive against odds very few had ever overcome. He could do this.

The woman glanced at the other one like her, the one still on her horse who'd ridden closer but not as near as the first. "Lola has a child of her own. She could nurse Pretty Shield, at least once to fill her belly until we decide what to do."

He studied that one. She looked surprised but then offered a hesitant nod. "I can do that." She might have a babe hidden beneath the trade blanket wrapped across her front.

As though she could hear his thoughts, she lifted one side of the covering to reveal a cradleboard tied around her. Inside was a babe not very different from his own, tiny and with a tuft of black hair.

Not a white babe.

He jerked his focus back up to the mother's face. She was definitely white. Which meant this infant had been stolen too. A fresh round of anger seeped through him. He would never allow her to touch Pretty Shield. He would find another way.

A motion from the village snatched his focus. He turned as a brave walked from between two lodges onto the grassland toward the woman and babe.

Goes Ahead tensed. This was no white man, though his hair wasn't cut like that of the Sioux.

"He is my husband." The woman with the child spoke up, as though to stop Goes Ahead from acting. "His name is White Owl. He is not one of those who did this terrible thing."

White Owl eyed Goes Ahead, though he continued walking toward the woman who said she was his. "I am Shoshone. We travel with the missionaries to help speak their message to the People. We are peaceful. To help." But the way he crowded beside the woman and rested a hand on her legging showed a protectiveness that did not match with peace.

The warrior did look Shoshone, and those people were not enemies of Goes Ahead's tribe, the White Clay People. Or the Gros Ventre, as these white strangers called them. But if he was traveling with these whites, had married one of them, his heart might have turned bad. Of course, if the babe the woman held was truly his child, it probably hadn't been stolen. Could it be safe to let her feed his hungry daughter? Pretty Shield's cries had become desperate, clutching at his heart in a way he wouldn't be able to bear much longer. But he could endure it for her safety.

"Please." The first woman, the one who'd walked toward him, looked a little desperate herself as she watched Pretty Shield's flailing arms. She didn't step closer again, but her hands lifted as though she wanted to take the babe.

He had to do something. Had to choose. Now.

He looked to the mother once more. Perhaps he could hold her child while she nursed his. That way she wouldn't be tempted to steal away with his daughter.

She met his gaze with a concerned look. "I'll sit right there on the ground and nurse her. And I'll give her back to you as soon as she's taken her fill."

That was nearly what he'd been thinking. Except for one detail. "I hold your child."

A flash of something close to terror crossed her face, and the brave beside her straightened. He shook his head. "No."

This, Goes Ahead could not back down on. If the woman was to take his babe from him, he would have her child to make sure she took care with his. His daughter needed to eat soon though. He couldn't risk losing the chance for her. Should he simply allow it?

What if they took her?

The woman placed her hand on the Shoshone brave's shoulder and spoke to him quietly. The two exchanged words, and she seemed to be pleading with him.

At last, she straightened and looked at Goes Ahead with a nod. "I know you will take care with our Anna, as I will with your Pretty Shield." She slid from her horse, the brave helping her lower with the cradle board.

Then they walked toward him, the Shoshone brave and the white woman carrying a babe that looked as native as any he'd seen. Who were these strange people?

He stayed still as they approached. The trees provided

shelter from the sun, and she could sit on the rise of ground beside him.

When she nearly reached him, she pulled the cradle board away from her body, then lifted it so the babe within the frame lay flat across her arms. She held her child out to him. "Please try not to jostle her. She's finally gone to sleep and will be hungry when she wakes. This way, I can feed your daughter as much as she needs before my own begins to cry for a meal."

He slipped his tomahawk back in its sheath and took the bundle in one arm, but relinquishing Pretty Shield in her bright red trade blanket was like standing exposed to a line of enemies with their arrows drawn. How could he give over his daughter?

He clenched his jaw as he allowed the woman to take her. She nestled his daughter close, bouncing and speaking soothing words while she sat. Pretty Shield's cries changed, though they didn't lessen. At last, they faded into suckling sounds while his daughter partook of what she so desperately needed.

The mother sat quietly with her, and the tension coiled inside him gradually began to ease. At least to the point that he could breathe fully. Her Shoshone husband stood on her other side, and the white man and woman had approached to stand near as well. None held rifles, though they surely had other weapons strapped to them.

The first woman, the one who'd spoken of Bright Eyes, broke their quiet. "She'll need to eat often. Do you have a plan? You can come with us to our next village if you'd like."

He tried to make sense of her words. Were they and the Sioux planning to attack another camp? He should stop them, but could he do that without putting his children at risk?

The man beside her spoke this time. "We are missionaries. We've come to tell the tribes about the one true God. We've been staying in this Salish village for about two moons to share of God's love for them." A sadness that was nearly believable took over his features, though it must be feigned. "We left two days ago to visit the camp we stayed in last. We never expected to return to this." He turned toward the lodges that hid so much bloodshed.

Goes Ahead could no longer look that direction. He couldn't let grief or anger distract him from guarding his child.

The man turned back to him. "My name is Ben Lane, and this is my sister Elise." He motioned to the woman with the sharp eyes and the insistent tongue.

His sister. For some reason, Goes Ahead had assumed they were man and wife.

Ben Lane motioned to the Shoshone and the woman nursing Pretty Shield. "You've already met White Owl, and this is his wife, Lola, and their daughter Anna. As my sister said, you're welcome to go with us to the next village where we'll bide, though we hadn't decided where to go from here. But we might go north, as we were traveling before."

The woman sitting on the ground—Lola—looked up at Goes Ahead, a bit of shyness in her gaze. "I can nurse her as long as I need to. I'm sure with both the babes eating, my supply will increase quickly."

Not all of the words they spoke were clear to him. Especially *missionary* and the entire picture of what exactly they were doing in each village. They'd not mentioned the Sioux, but they probably wouldn't speak of a secret connection with them.

He couldn't go with these people, but one thing had come clear in his mind. He needed this woman, Lola.

His only choice was to take his children across the mountains to the village he'd grown up in, to the people he'd been so relieved to leave before he married Bright Eyes and moved into her Salish village. Now, that was his best option. He could only protect his children alone for so long. He needed the help of his tribe. And apparently, he needed this woman to help him get there.

He eyed the other three who watched him. Without their

rifles aimed at him, he could cut them all down and force the mother to come. The thought only made his belly churn more. Too much bloodshed had happened here already. And to kill a woman—it went against everything inside him.

But if it was necessary to protect his children?

"Do you have family?" Elise spoke again. "We could help you take Pretty Shield to another village if you have someone there to help."

She seemed earnest, though she likely didn't realize the journey would require crossing the mountains in the midst of the cold months. Very few attempted that trek, and he wouldn't consider it with his children now if it wasn't so important to reach the safety of his village.

Did he dare allow all these people to come? Perhaps the mountains and the cold would eliminate them for him.

But what if they tried to steal his children and escape before the journey proved too treacherous for them? He would have to be watchful. Always on his guard, never letting his son and daughter out of his sight.

This he could do. He had the strength and cunning to protect these two who were all he had left. Especially if that meant his tiny babe would have food until they reached the help of his family.

He addressed the group. "I go to my people over the mountains." He motioned toward the peaks they would have to climb. "You come on the journey." He focused his gaze on the mother. "Feed Pretty Shield. I will give you gift of horses. Warm furs." As long as they didn't try to take his children from him along the way. If they attempted it, they would receive nothing except the blade of his tomahawk.

Though the mother nodded, it was Elise who answered. "We don't need any gifts, but we would be happy to go with you and help with the baby." She paused for a second, then seemed to hesitate. "Your...son? You said you won him back. Is he already with your people?"

Why was she so focused on Walking Bird? He would have to watch this one very close.

"I will bring him here before we lay the dead ones to rest. When sun rises tomorrow, we leave this place."

When he came here five winters before and accepted the trade with Bright Eyes's father to marry her, he would never have imagined he'd be leaving with only their two children— and white people he didn't trust.

CHAPTER 3

"*E*lise, have you taken leave of your senses?"

Elise raised her brows at her brother as he plowed a hand through his unruly curls, then plopped his hat back on his head.

She gave him her most certain smile. "Don't you see? God brought him to us. Brought us back to the village at the very moment he was here. If we'd come even an hour later, he might have already left with Pretty Shield." Certainty pressed in her chest. *Thank You for using us to aid this man, Lord.*

She glanced over her shoulder in the direction the brave had disappeared minutes before. Who knew how long they had before he returned with his son? And *would* he return? He had too. *Please, Lord.* His daughter needed to eat, and Lola would be the only source of food for at least a day's ride. Since the babe had a full belly now, would he think he had time to reach another village? Surely he wouldn't put Pretty Shield through that misery. *Please, Lord.*

Why did this particular infant's plight raise such desperation in her? Because the babe's mother had been kind to Elise. And because of the atrocity done to the entire village. That must be it.

She had to lay the matter in God's hands and trust that the Lord would bring the brave and his tiny daughter—and his son —back to them as he'd promised. And she had to overcome her brother's skepticism before then. White Owl's, too, from the look of him.

Beside her, Lola spoke, her voice quieter than normal. "I'm glad we can help keep his baby alive until he reaches his family."

"I think he'll steal you away and leave the rest of us for dead the first chance he finds." White Owl nearly growled the words.

Elise couldn't blame him for being protective of his young family, but this was the perfect chance to show White Owl God's love in action. He'd matured in the faith so much since his conversion last summer, but everyone needed an occasional reminder.

She rested a hand on Lola's arm as she addressed White Owl. "It seemed to me he was more concerned about his daughter and son than us. Imagine the pain he must be feeling, having had his son kidnapped from their own village. Then just when he gets him safely home and thinks they can finally be a family again, he returns to find his dear wife murdered. And all their friends. He only has his children left. It makes sense he would be grieving and angry, though he did try not to let us see the depth of his emotions. He needs God's love now more than perhaps ever before in his life. And we can be the hands and feet of that love, helping to care for his children and ease his burden as much as we can."

White Owl didn't look happy about the thought, but he seemed far less determined against it now. Hopefully her speech had softened her brother, as well.

She slid a glance his way. "Right, Benji?"

His mouth formed a firm line, though not pressed thin like he was angry. Her brother had just as much desire to share the

Lord with these people as she did, but he let his protectiveness hold him back at times. Lord willing, this would *not* be one of those moments.

No one spoke, and as silence threatened to hover among them, she turned her attention to the grim work they had to complete before they could leave. "I suppose we need to start preparing graves." Her throat ached with the words, and tears burned her eyes again. This was not what she'd envisioned back when she'd been planning their journey of service to the Indians.

But she and Ben had committed to do even the hard things to reach these people. She had no idea whether the two months they'd dwelled in this village had impacted the final destinations of these souls, but at least she and Ben could give their bodies the reverence due God's beloved creation.

As she helped walk through the village in search of tools to dig with, her gorge rose up into her throat. She tried not to look at the lifeless faces, the blood sprayed on blankets and lodge walls.

And the eyes. The cold, lifeless gazes of people she'd spoken with and eaten with and laughed with only days before. By the time they found enough sharp tools to begin the job of digging graves, her body had gone numb, her mind along with it. White Owl had insisted Lola stay with the horses and care for Anna, so at least her friend was spared these images.

Elise's pain must have showed on her face, for when she brought Ben the tools she found, he took one look at her and shook his head. "We found a gully where we can lay the bodies and cover them with rocks. I think that will protect them from animals best, especially when snow layers over the stones through the winter." He pointed upriver. "It's just beyond those trees. Go gather as many rocks as you can. White Owl and I will bring the people to bury."

She didn't have the fortitude to argue with him. It wasn't fair for Ben to have to face such devastation either. But she might not last much longer if she had to handle the lifeless forms of friends. These were only the outer shells, as the souls had already left. Yet it was the thought of the final destination of those souls that brought the most angst.

Lord, why didn't we come to this place sooner? We could have convinced them to accept Your love.

She left the village and followed the river in the direction Ben had pointed. This was the way Pretty Shield's father had gone to retrieve his son. The man hadn't even told them his name.

The gully was easy enough to find, and the area already possessed a number of smaller stones, but they would need more. How many people would there be to bury? At least twenty. Nay, closer to thirty. This had been a small village, but such a happy one.

The sting of tears pressed harder, and now that she was alone, she let the drops fall as she worked. One rock at a time, she gathered from an ever-widening circle and brought them back to the gully. The sharp edges cut her hands, their weight chipped her nails, and her back ached with the bending. But those discomforts were little compared to the pain inside, and nothing at all considering what these precious people had endured.

The sound of something walking through the trees nearby brought her upright, and she blinked to pull herself from her thoughts. They'd been told there were no bear west of the Rockies, but the time she'd nearly stumbled on a grizzly on the eastern side of the mountains still made her blood run cold. Only the ingenuity of the native women she'd been gathering berries with had saved them from certain attack.

She had no such help this time. Only her own wits and aching muscles.

The flash of brown fur that appeared between the trees

made her body coil. She dropped the rock and took a step back, but her gaze stayed riveted on the shadow passing between those trunks.

Then something paler flashed above the fur, too high to be a bear. Her throat loosened enough to let in air. Another glimpse showed more detail this time.

A man on horseback.

Her body relaxed, though perhaps it shouldn't, for he was riding her direction. She couldn't see well enough to make out whether this was Pretty Shield's father or not, only that he was an Indian riding a brown horse.

A break in the trees finally revealed him clearly. The babe's father. He wore a fur draped over his chest, loosely enough that it might be covering Pretty Shield.

But where was the boy he'd gone to retrieve?

A little face peeked out from behind the man, so cute and unexpected, and a small bit of weight lifted from her chest. The pair were twenty strides from her, and the lad stared at her with wide eyes and a solemn mouth. A shock of black hair framed his face.

She worked for a smile but couldn't quite manage it. Not with the smothering grief and the tightness of tears tugging her face. She would need to try harder. This boy had already endured so much. Did he know yet of his mother's passing?

The horse stopped a half-dozen steps from her, and the man looked from her to the gully behind her. Before, his eyes had been sharp, almost fiery. But now their dullness made the lump rise into her throat again.

Did he have specific plans for his wife's body? He'd said *lay the dead to rest*, but the Salish customs to accomplish that might be very different than the English.

Lord, don't let our actions bring him more pain.

She motioned toward the gathered stones. "We were preparing a grave for the bodies so they would be safe from

CALM IN THE MOUNTAIN STORM

animals. Ben and White Owl will be bringing them soon. If you'd rather do something different..." Hopefully, he understood her meaning. He'd showed a remarkable grasp of English so far.

He nodded, his gaze still on the dip in the ground. Even from here, she could see the way his throat worked.

Then he turned his horse and rode toward the village without a word. That nod seemed to say that he approved their plan. Perhaps he was going to bring his wife's body himself.

She reached down for the rock she'd dropped and carried it to lay with the others, but her mind strayed to where Pretty Shield's father was probably dismounting by the village and helping the boy down. What would he do with the children while he worked? That sober-faced lad couldn't have been more than four or five years old. Allowing him to see the carnage around his home—especially his mother's body—would be unthinkable.

Her feet turned to follow after them before her mind had the chance to say *yay* or *nay*.

When the village came in sight, she saw that the man had halted near the same trees where he'd been standing before, a short distance away from where Lola nursed little Anna.

Man and boy had dismounted, and both crouched over something in the grass. Pretty Shield?

She continued their direction. He might not wish for her interference, but she'd like to meet the lad, Bright Eyes's son. And she could offer to hold Pretty Shield while the brave did what he needed to in the village. Part of her craved to snuggle the tiny bundle against her, to cherish the sweet trusting cherub.

The father looked as she approached, and she slowed her steps and worked for a smile. "I came to meet your son and tell you I can help with the children while you...take care of things." Perhaps it was overly selfish of her to ask for such a pleasant task while the men tended to the hardest work of all.

He didn't answer but turned to the boy and spoke. Though his words were almost too quiet for her to understand, they sounded like one of the native languages. Had the boy learned English, or would he only speak Salish?

His father turned back to the tiny babe nestled inside her bright red blanket. He hadn't answered her question, though she hadn't really spoken in the form of a query, had she? He didn't tell her *no*, so perhaps she was safe to approach.

The boy watched her as she drew near, his eyes wide and round, though not from alarm, as far as she could tell. They were beautiful, intelligent, and wary eyes.

When she came within a few steps, she stopped and crouched low to be closer to his level. "Hello. I am called Elise." She touched her fingers to her chest as she spoke, then pointed to him. "What is your name?"

He gave no sign he understood, just watched her with those impossibly wide eyes and the solemn pinch to his mouth. Then those lips opened. "Walking Bird."

A true smile rose up inside her. He *had* understood. And he was actually speaking with her. Part of her had wondered if the trauma he'd endured might keep him quiet. What a strong little boy.

She gave him a bright look. "I'm pleased to meet you, Walking Bird." She looked past him to the small arms and legs flailing among the cloth. Their father appeared to be changing her diaper. Did he have clean supplies? Most of the Salish used soft rabbit skins for diapers, with dry grass tucked inside to help absorb. With the blanket still tucked around the babe, she couldn't tell whether he was putting on or taking off.

She turned her attention back to the boy. "Is that your sister?"

Like before, he regarded her without a hint of understanding. Perhaps he'd only learned that simple introduction. But then he gave a firm nod.

She smiled at him again. "She's very pretty. While you and your Papa were away, sometimes I would sit with your Mama and hold your sister or change her soiled diapers." The boy surely didn't understand everything she said, but conversation of any kind would help them get to know each other.

She glanced at his father, though the man didn't look at her. He seemed to be fumbling with a knot in the rabbit skin, his large fingers spanning almost half the length of the baby's arm. "I can go find clean skins to replace her wrapping. Unless you have some already."

His response was a grunt, and his mouth pinched in a thin line as he continued to struggle. She itched to move closer and take over the task for him, but if he didn't already have clean diapers, obtaining them would be the first step. There was no sense taking off the wet if they had nothing dry to replace it with.

At last, he shook his head. "I only have blanket." The babe would need that for warmth. Her bare arms and legs must already be cold in the chilly wind.

She stood. "I'll go get some things for her." In the shock of seeing his wife and so many others murdered, his thought had probably only been to save his daughter's life, not to pack all the necessities she'd need on a journey through the mountains. Did he even know what a babe would require?

CHAPTER 4

*A*fter stopping to see if Lola needed anything as she nursed Anna, Elise made her way toward the lodge she knew to belong to Bright Eyes. Ben and White Owl had laid blankets over the bodies they hadn't yet moved, and she sent another heartsick prayer to the Lord as she skirted Bright Eyes's limp form and stepped into the hut.

A few food bundles and dishes lay by the coals of the cooking fire, but everything else in the home seemed to have been put neatly in its place. She'd come to sit with Bright Eyes and enjoy time with her and the babe twice, and if she remembered correctly, the woman had kept extra rabbit skins for diapers in one of the baskets at the foot of her sleeping pallet.

There. Not only a stack of the softest leather squares, but also two tiny gowns also made of the impossibly-smooth buckskin. She'd seen some of the women working hides to make them more supple, sometimes scraping them with sharp stones and sometimes chewing with their teeth. How long had Bright Eyes worked to craft such fine clothing?

She started to take the baby's things from the basket, but it might be easier just to bring the entire container. Her gaze flicked to the basket beside it—and caught on another item of small, well-made clothing. Though reaching for it felt like she was venturing into places not intended for her, she touched the garment and lifted it out.

A beautiful tunic, a little larger than the other. Probably the perfect size for a lad of about four years old. She riffled through the other contents in that basket, which all appeared to be clothing and toys for the boy. He would appreciate having them now.

After gathering a basket in each arm, she glanced around the place. There were a number of furs that their father might want to bring. And surely he had clothing and other personal items to pack, but he could come gather those himself.

Her gaze landed on the food packs by the fire. Two camas cakes lay fully baked on the bark plate, and a leather pouch held dried berries and baked camas root. The boy might be hungry, especially for his mother's cooking. She rolled the food in the hide and tucked it in one of the baskets.

As she made her way out of the lodge, through the village, and back to the little family clustered under the trees, she sent up a steady rhythm of prayers. *Let him be openhearted toward us. Comfort them both in their grief. Little Pretty Shield too. She won't understand why her mother's arms don't cradle her and offer the nourishment she needs. Help me to stand in her stead in every way possible.*

She set the baskets beside the children's father, then knelt next to him. He'd managed to work the second knot free and was just exposing the foul-smelling contents. He jerked back and turned away, losing all the solemn dignity he'd worn like a layer of skin.

Despite everything, she had to hold in a snort. "I can change her."

He pushed to his feet and stepped back nearly before she had the words out. She grinned as she shifted in front of the babe.

She laid a hand on one of the squirming little legs. "Hello, there. Let's get this soiled mess off of you." She kept up a singsong rhythm as Pretty Shield stared up at her with the same wide dark eyes as her brother. Bright Eyes had been a lovely woman, and her husband certainly possessed a handsome face. Together they'd conceived the most beautiful children Elise had ever seen.

The babe squirmed and fussed as she cleaned her, but once she had a dry diaper and her warm blanket snuggled around her again, Pretty Shield's fretting eased.

"There now." Elise lifted the bundle so the babe's ear rested against her chest. Cradling her close, she swayed back and forth, letting the age-old rhythm soothe the child. "That's a girl. There's our sweet girl. You're safe and loved. God loves you. I love you. Your Papa loves you. Your brother loves you."

The lad was watching her, and when she spoke of him, she sent him a wink.

A bit of emotion sparked in his eyes for the first time—a hint of a smile that spread over his mouth. If he would ever truly grin, he would be so precious she might not be able to deny him anything.

Their father looked on from a few steps away. She still had no idea what to call him, but now didn't seem the time to ask his name.

She reached for the basket that held Walking Bird's things. "I brought a few special treasures for you." After slipping her hand under the clothing, she pulled out the first item her fingers found. "What is this?"

What indeed? It was a block of some sort, colored on each side and carved with pictures. When she held it up, his eyes lit with eagerness. He reached out, but his hand stopped midway between them, as though he knew better than to snatch it. Had he learned that hesitation during his kidnapping? Or was it simply good manners his parents had instilled in him?

She held the toy out the rest of the way and placed the piece in his tiny grip. His mouth flashed white teeth as he studied several of the pictures. Then his gaze found hers. "More."

Wasn't it funny how children were always looking for something better? She matched his grin and reached into the basket again. When she extracted the next item, it was another painted block, but with different carvings.

His smile stretched his cheeks as he took it from her. That must be what he meant by *more*. Not something better, just the rest of his collection.

One by one, she pulled out toys—three more blocks, then a round thing shaped almost like a top. He focused on lining up the pieces with a precision most lads his age wouldn't worry over.

With him distracted, she returned her attention to the babe snuggled against her chest. Pretty Shield seemed content now, and Elise rested her cheek on the tuft of soft black hair poking out from the blanket. "A sweet girl you are."

As she soaked in the moment, awareness prickled over her. Their father still stood nearby watching. She'd been so focused on the children, she'd forgotten his presence.

Lifting her head from the babe's, she turned a sheepish smile on him. "I can stay with them if you have things you need to do."

His intense gaze studied her. What was he thinking behind those dark eyes? Was it simply her white skin he didn't trust? Or did grief make him cling tighter to his children than a father usually did?

She held his gaze. "We won't move from this place."

He stared at her another long minute before finally giving a single nod. "I will be always nearby."

As he turned toward the village, she finally had the presence of mind to remember what she'd meant to ask before. "Wait."

He stilled, then turned slowly to look at her. The careful movement intensified the feeling of strength he exuded. She swallowed to bring moisture back into her mouth. "Will you tell me your name?"

"*Ba'suck'osh*. I am called Goes Ahead." Then he turned away from her and resumed his former path.

She tasted the words, both the English and the interpretation in his language. Ba'suck'osh. Was that Salish? The village he'd come from was across the Rockies, so it was likely a different tribe. But which one? So many questions she had for this man. Maybe on their journey, she could find the courage to ask.

～

*T*his little boy had far more personality than Elise had credited him with when they'd first met.

She grinned as she rode beside her brother the next day along the winding mountain path. Goes Ahead led their group and had his infant daughter strapped to his front. His son sat behind him, and the lad hadn't stopped moving since they started out three hours before.

When they passed trees, he would reach out and snag leaves or branches. More than once, he'd held the end as long as he could while the horse plodded forward, and when he'd finally released the tip, it sprang back to slap Elise or her brother.

After the first time, she learned to catch the leaves before they hit her.

When no trees provided distraction, he squirmed, sometimes rocking from side to side, swooping with his arms as though he was an eagle soaring, or drawing back on an imaginary bow. With all the wiggles, he came dangerously close to leaning off the horse more than once.

Much of the time, Goes Ahead kept a hand clamped on the boy's knee, but when the babe began to fuss, he had to release the lad to focus on her. Good thing his mount stayed steady.

Would Goes Ahead allow Elise to take one of the children? Perhaps, although he'd kept them both at his side since he finished burying his wife yesterday. He'd only allowed Lola to take the babe when she fussed strongly enough there was no doubt of her hunger. Which had been often, since Lola's milk still hadn't increased enough to satisfy both babes.

Elise could understand his need to keep his children close, but such a tight grip would wear him out before the week's end. Maybe she could ease him into the idea of sharing his load.

When the trail widened, she moved her gelding up alongside his horse. While Goes Ahead barely sent her a glance, his son regarded her with those beautiful wide eyes. She sent him a smile before looking at Pretty Shield. A blanket covered her against the wind, so she looked like only a lump beneath the bright red cloth.

She lifted her gaze to Goes Ahead's profile. "Would it help if one of the children rides with me? I could occupy Walking Bird or try to put the babe to sleep. That way you only have one to manage."

At the sound of her voice, the form beneath the blanket began to squirm, making the cloth poke out at various angles that were probably her hands or feet. Goes Ahead frowned down, looking beneath the covering. "She had finally settled until you spoke."

Surely the babe didn't recognize her voice. It must have been only the sound that made her stir. Elise extended a hand. "Perhaps if I sing to her, she'll fall asleep. I'll ride right here beside you."

His brows stayed scrunched in that frown, but he finally lifted the sling holding his daughter. Relief slipped through Elise as they halted the horses and she took the wee bundle from him. The babe waved her arms as though struggling until Elise pulled her close, raising her up so one tiny ear rested over Elise's heartbeat. She swayed a little in the saddle as she tucked her chin over Pretty Shield's head. "There, sweet one. You're safe and loved." The babe quieted instantly, and a little tremor slipped through her, as though breathing out the last of her angst.

Oh, this precious bundle. Such a tiny gift from God, too young to understand how her life had changed. Yet she no doubt felt the upheaval nonetheless.

If only Elise could stay in this position forever, but she had to fasten the sling over her shoulder before they could begin riding again. After lifting her head, she twisted to bring the ends together to tie. Yet with one arm holding the child secure, she would never be able to manage a knot with the other hand.

She caught Walking Bird watching her, so she raised her brows at him. "Will you tie this on for me?"

He ducked his chin but couldn't hide the tug of his lips. Almost a smile even.

His father grunted and reached toward her. She caught her breath but leaned closer and handed him the two ends. The touch of their fingers in the exchange was enough to send her pulse pounding, but as his hands brushed her shoulder repeatedly while he fastened the knot, she could neither breathe nor move.

Who would have ever thought this strong brave would be fastening an infant sling on her? In truth, he looked like the kind of man who would spend all his time hunting and doing what warriors did, not bothering himself with the children.

Had he been like that before? Before his son was kidnapped from beneath his wife's nose. Had he been away when Walking Bird was taken? Or nearby talking with the other village men? She couldn't quite form a picture of who this man was separate from the tragedy that surrounded him now.

At last, he finished securing the tie and she straightened, sending him a smile of thanks. She couldn't quite meet his gaze though.

They rode on in quiet, especially as Walking Bird finally tired and slumped against his father's back for a nap. In her arms, Pretty Shield did the same, her tiny bowed lips parted as she breathed. So peaceful.

She dared a look at their father. He rode straight-backed, despite the fact that he had no saddle or stirrups. She was no master horseman, but when she'd been a girl, her father would sometimes lift them up on his cart horse's bare back and lead them around the yard. Even now, she could remember how tired her body became after riding only a short time without stirrups. Goes Ahead must be built almost entirely of lean muscle to hold himself as he did.

She worked for a light tone. "Your family we're traveling to, are they Salish also?"

He shook his head, though he didn't look at her. "The White Clay people. You may know them as Gros Ventre."

"Ahh." She'd heard of the Gros Ventre. In fact... "I think Ben and I may have met some of your people when we first came west. A small band near the Missouri River." The natives called that river something different, but she couldn't remember their name. Perhaps he would know it by the English title also.

Now he slid her a look. "The White Clay people move with the hunting. When did you see these?"

"It would have been spring a year ago." Was there a chance she'd met his family? Or perhaps he and Bright Eyes had lived with his kin back then. She would remember them if she'd met either of them before, surely. But she and Ben hadn't stayed with the band, only spent an afternoon talking with them around a campfire.

He must be trying to determine the same, for he shook his head. "I do not know if our people camped near the great river then."

Perhaps she could venture a few more questions that seemed

more personal, since he'd begun talking. "When did you and Bright Eyes move to this village?"

He didn't answer right away, just kept his focus ahead. Had she pressed too far? Memories of his murdered wife would be painful.

But then he answered. "Five summers ago. I came across the mountains with three warriors from my village. Her father offered much in trade. Ten horses. Good lodge."

She couldn't stop herself from staring at him as her mind sorted what he'd just said. Marrying had been a business deal? She knew that practice could be common among the natives. But in her mind, Bright Eyes and this man had been a love match. Had that depth of connection eventually grown between them? Surely it had after five years and two children.

But what was love anyway? Young girls thought of the notion with fanciful imaginings, but she wasn't sure she'd ever seen that type of romantic affection played out in real life. Certainly not with her own parents. Even long before they raised twelve children, if love existed between her father and mother, they displayed it in such mundane traits as duty and consistency and reliability.

Perhaps that had been the case with Bright Eyes and Goes Ahead. But had the heart of the strong brave riding beside her become involved?

Of course she couldn't ask him. But there was another question raised by his comment that she might chance. "Had you planned to leave your village permanently? What of the others who came with you?" It made sense he would have stayed among her people once they wed. After all, the Bible said the man should leave his father and mother and be joined to his wife. But had he set out to find a wife? Or simply for an adventure?

Again he was silent. Perhaps she really had pressed too far this time. But maybe he was simply giving thought to his answer, for he didn't sound annoyed when he spoke. "We left the People, all four of us. When I became Salish, the others rode on toward the setting sun."

She tipped her head at him, making her voice light and a little teasing. "Seeking adventure? Or hoping to find a marriage trade half so good as yours?" She was playing with fire, jesting in such a way with this brave.

But the tiniest hint of a smile touched his mouth. Perhaps it was only wishful thinking on her part or a trick of the sunlight.

He didn't answer though, and the steady swish of the horses' hooves in the grass filled the air between them.

The quiet gave her too much time to ponder why he and those other men had left the Gros Ventre village. Had something happened to force them out? Had conditions been so hard they thought it best to set out to make their own fortunes?

And would whatever caused his departure affect how he was welcomed on his return?

CHAPTER 5

*G*oes Ahead needed some distance from these people. They weren't at all how he'd expected. Not spiteful or secretive. Elise did press harder than the others, talking to him often as they rode. Sometimes her words were only about necessary things, but other times she asked question after question about the journey or the land they rode through. Her curiosity didn't grate on his nerves as much as he would have expected. Even the most probing questions came with a gentleness that set aside his guard.

What *did* stretch his control to the outermost limit was the squirming and whining of his son. The boy never stopped moving, even in his sleep. Twice, he'd slumped against Goes Ahead's back as the exhaustion overcame him, but even then, his little body twitched often.

He'd not been such a challenge after Goes Ahead had first stolen him back from the Sioux. The boy had mostly clung to him as though if he let go, he might be taken again.

But now... Perhaps Walking Bird had been riding for too many days in a row. Or maybe he simply missed his mother. He certainly asked about her aplenty.

Guilt pressed in Goes Ahead's chest. He still had to tell him the truth. He'd only said Bright Eyes wasn't at their village, that no one was there and that was why they had to ride farther across the mountains. Soon, he would need to explain that they would never see her again, at least not until they all reached the Big Sand after death.

He shouldn't have waited this long to speak of it. Hard things had to be faced. It would make a warrior of his son to learn this now. But so soon after what those Sioux dogs did to him, when Goes Ahead had looked into his son's wary eyes to tell him those same snakes had also cut down his mother…he'd not been able to speak the words.

He eyed the growing darkness, then turned his horse toward a cluster of trees. They should stop now. The woman, Lola, had nursed his daughter not long ago, so this fussing shouldn't be from hunger. Probably her rabbit skin needed dry grass. Had the babe really needed to be changed so often before? He couldn't think of a full day he'd spent in her presence to know for certain, but he'd never thought so. No wonder Bright Eyes complained of getting little done when the babes were little.

He halted at the edge of the trees and spoke in the white man's tongue. "Camp here." Then he spoke to his son in the Atsina language that would be used in the village where they were going. "Take my hand to climb from the horse. You will come with me to water and tie him."

Even as Walking Bird gripped Goes Ahead's wrist and slid to the ground, he switched to Salish and took on that awful whining tone again. "I'm tired. I don't want to water."

Goes Ahead worked to keep his frustration from showing, but he didn't release the boy's hand when he tried to squirm away. He'd been too lax with his son, not teaching him to speak as the White Clay people did. Now they would both be judged for that lack. But at least Walking Bird had a little longer to learn. If only he would stop this laziness.

Goes Ahead tugged the boy forward as he spoke in Atsina again. "A warrior cares for his horse before himself."

"No."

He had to clamp his jaw against that frustrating tone. The horse walked along much easier than the boy.

By the time they'd settled the animal and returned to the place where the others were gathering, Pretty Shield had begun to fuss again. Lola was already nursing her own babe, and Elise worked to build a fire. White Owl had still been hobbling their horses, and Ben carried packs to the campsite.

As soon as Goes Ahead released his son's hand, the boy collapsed onto the grass. "I'm too tired. I don't know why I have to work. I want to play with my toy."

Goes Ahead didn't dare ease his jaw enough to speak, lest he lose the last bit of his control. No warrior had ever been tested so, surely. Not even running an enemy gauntlet proved as hard to endure as the unrelenting cries of these two children.

When he laid the packs and bedding near the fire, Elise gave him an assessing look. Without a word, she stood and moved toward him, then reached into the sling at his chest and took out Pretty Shield. The babe quieted immediately as Elise raised her to her shoulder.

Then the woman turned to his son. "Will you help me freshen your sister's diaper? I need you to make silly faces to distract her while I work. After that, I bet I can gather more sticks for the fire than you can."

Just like his daughter had, Walking Bird instantly stopped fussing. He straightened, and his eyes lit.

At last, she turned to Goes Ahead, and her tone changed from the playful cadence she used with his children to her usual voice. "If you'll hand me her pack, I'll get her cleaned up."

He shouldn't allow this woman to take over with his children, but clearly his strength wasn't as great as he'd thought. He pulled out the bundle that contained fresh rabbit skins and

CALM IN THE MOUNTAIN STORM

clothing for Pretty Shield, then stepped back. "I will get firewood."

She glanced up from where she and Walking Bird were already unfastening the babe's soiled things. The knowing glint in her eyes didn't look as much like censure as understanding. "We'll be fine here."

For the first time in two days, he could believe that would be true. With a nod and a hushed sigh of relief, he turned and stepped into the trees.

$\approx$

*A*nother yawn forced Elise's jaw wide as she pulled her saddle's cinch strap tight the next morning. She patted her gelding's neck, then led him toward the rest of the group.

White Owl had already mounted, his daughter's cradleboard strapped to him. Lola fussed with the blanket over little Anna so it protected the babe from the much colder temperature they'd awakened to today. When her friend finally turned to mount her own mare, Lola's sleepy eyes couldn't be missed. Her milk supply was still catching up to provide enough to nurse both babes, which meant she'd had to feed them each several times in the night. These challenging days would pass soon enough. They simply had to push through.

Elise and White Owl had helped as much as they could, changing wet diapers and soothing fussy infants while the babes waited their turn. She'd told Goes Ahead it would be best if he stayed with his son so the boy didn't wake, which hopefully meant both of them were rested for the challenges today would bring.

The man wouldn't have been able to sleep through all the infant's fussing though. At least one time, she'd heard Walking Bird's little voice speaking to his father in their language. The tone hadn't been the same frustrating whine as before but had been small and uncertain. He was probably missing his mother. Had Goes Ahead told him the truth? The boy didn't mourn as though he realized she's passed away. But then, how well could a four-year-old understand death?

Goes Ahead approached, leading his stallion with his daughter's sling tied around him and his son scampering along at his side. The boy looked fully invigorated, nothing left of his exhaustion from the end of yesterday's ride. Which meant he would be full of energy in the saddle again.

Perhaps Goes Ahead would allow the rest of them to help with the boy today. He'd let her take Pretty Shield several times yesterday afternoon.

She gave them all a smile, then honed her focus on Walking Bird. "Are you ready to ride?"

The lad scrunched his nose and shook his head vehemently. The reaction brought a frown to his father's face, but Elise smiled to keep the tone light. "Perhaps he could ride behind my saddle or my brother's as we start out. We can shift him from one person to another as he grows tired. That way the day goes easier for all."

Her words tightened Goes Ahead's frown still more. He looked down at his son and seemed to move closer to him. As much as that overly-strong protective instinct frustrated her, she could understand the reason behind it. He'd nearly lost this boy. He wouldn't allow him to go far. Not for a while, anyway.

She gentled her voice and worked to make things easier for him. "If you prefer, he can start out with you, then move to one of our horses as he grows restless."

Was that relief that eased the man's features? He nodded... progress enough for now.

She stood nearby in case he needed help mounting with the children, but even with the babe strapped around his front, he pulled himself up on his horse with no sign of effort. Then he reached down and hoisted up his son with one arm.

The boy landed with a squirming bounce, as though already trying to nudge the stallion forward. His father rested a staying hand on his knee as he spoke in a low voice. Too bad she didn't yet know the language.

If only she had a better aptitude for learning. White Owl had been trying to teach her both the sign language and the Salish tongue all summer. She could communicate somewhat with the hand talk, but no matter how many Salish words she learned in his slow, measured instruction, when native speakers began to talk, she could glean almost none of their meaning. What Goes Ahead spoke now didn't even seem to be the same sounds she'd been learning in Salish.

His gaze lifted to her, catching her staring. She offered a sheepish smile, then turned back to look for her brother. She needed to let him know of her hopes for the boy to ride with them. Ben would be glad for the chance to help, she had no doubt. He still stood with his horse where they'd saddled, fidgeting with one of the packs.

She lifted her voice to reach him. "Come on, Benjamin. We're wasting precious daylight." And the short good-behavior time of the young ones.

Her brother looked up and grinned. "Coming. Just wanted to make sure everything was secure." He tugged a strap tight, then gathered his reins and swung into the saddle.

They started off much as they had the day before, with Goes Ahead in the lead, Ben and her riding next, then White Owl and Lola behind. When they left the shelter of the trees, the wind began to whip in earnest, plunging its icy fingers between all the cracks in her attire—between her scarf and neck, under her coat sleeves, and even through the seams in the trousers she wore beneath her skirt. Her nose ran incessantly, and it was surely bright red from rubbing.

She glanced back at Lola and little Anna to make sure they were well-protected. Her friend wore a coat made of buffalo skin, a gift from White Owl, no doubt. The babe still nestled in the cradle board at her father's chest, but he'd covered her with a thick wolf hide. The females in White Owl's care were clearly well-protected.

She turned forward again to study Goes Ahead's children. He'd wrapped an animal skin over Pretty Shield, too, so she should be plenty sheltered. Walking Bird wore a coat of fur, but its fit had become nearly too small for him, with his hands and wrists peeking out and nothing on his head. She knew well how quickly children grew out of clothing. Her own mother spent more hours than Elise could count in the rocking chair of an evening. When Mama wasn't nursing babes, she would be sewing—letting out seams or taking in clothing to be handed down to the next child in line. Elise and Wendy, her next sister down, had the jobs of keeping the children occupied and meals on the table at the right time. Wendy had usually preferred to tuck herself away in the kitchen, so Elise learned to be creative with games and distractions for the little ones.

It appeared Walking Bird needed both entertainment and something to keep his exposed limbs warm.

The horses climbed a rocky slope at an angle, toward a pass between this small mountain and the one beside them. As soon as the terrain allowed, she nudged her gelding up near Goes Ahead's. "Is this a good time to let Walking Bird ride with Ben? I also have an extra fur he might like to wrap around himself since the weather is cold now."

Goes Ahead looked back at his son and only hesitated a moment before nodding. He spoke a few words to the boy, then reined to a halt.

She glanced back at Ben to make sure her brother rode near to get the boy. He reined his horse around hers and approached close enough to reach out and grip Walking Bird under the arms.

The lad's grin widened as Ben swung him through the air

and landed him with a plop on his own horse's neck, facing back toward the tail. "There you go, fella. You can ride just like that."

Walking Bird gripped the saddle horn, his smile wide, but he shook his head in such a precious way.

Ben chuckled. "You'd rather face forward? Maybe sit on something a little sturdier than ol' Billy's neck?"

With that same precious smile, Walking Bird nodded.

"If you say so." Ben gripped the boy under his arms and hoisted him back into the air and around to settle behind the saddle. "You can have a nice comfortable spot on top of my bed roll. Just hold on tight to my sides."

She glanced at Goes Ahead to see what he thought of her brother's teasing. His face gave no hint of his opinion, though he watched them intently.

At last, Ben turned to Goes Ahead with a nod. "I think we're ready. Looks like snow might fall any minute."

She jerked her gaze to the sky. Thick gray clouds pressed low, but she'd seen the same several times in the past weeks, and snow hadn't fallen yet. Though she'd been in this land nearly a year and a half, she still hadn't learned to read the signs for weather.

She glanced from her brother to Goes Ahead. "How do you know when it will snow?"

Ben paused a moment, probably to see if Goes Ahead would answer. When he didn't, her brother finally spoke. "For me, I think it's a combination of the low dark clouds like this, that really icy feel in the air, and something I can smell." He shrugged. "It's hard to explain. Goes Ahead or White Owl might have a better way of saying it."

She would look to White Owl for an answer soon, but perhaps their leader would share his experience. She turned to Goes Ahead.

He didn't glance at them, nor at the sky. Instead, he scanned the low trees that dotted the slope farther down. "It is the same as your brother said. And I watch the animals. The rabbits have found cover. The birds hide instead of calling to each other."

He'd really been watching to notice what the rabbits and birds were doing as they traversed these mountain trails?

She glanced at White Owl for his answer to her question, but he merely shrugged, nodding toward Goes Ahead as if to say, *His answer is mine too.*

Goes Ahead turned his horse the direction they'd been traveling. "Ride now."

They set out again, Ben moving his mare in behind Goes Ahead's stallion so the boy would stay near his father. Walking Bird bounced and swayed with the horse's gait, but she could see Ben pointing and hear the low hum of his voice as he spoke. The boy pointed back, and this time his squirming seemed more intentional, mostly excitement from whatever her brother said.

Ben had a way with children. You couldn't grow up in such a large family without developing that skill.

Something wet touched her cheek, and she shifted her focus to the air in front of her. "Look! A snowflake. The snow is starting."

No matter how old she grew, she would never lose the thrill of the first few snowflakes back in Illinois. In their little hometown of Marcyville, all the children within walking distance would bring their sleds—or simply their bundled self—to the hill behind the parsonage. Most of the land was either flat or tree covered, but that one hill provided the perfect snow pleasure ground. While waiting their turn to sled, the youngsters built forts and people from the icy crystals, or simply pelted each other with snowballs. The hillside rang with laughter for days.

She nudged her horse up as close as she could to Ben's mount on the narrow trail. "Walking Bird, did you see the snowflakes?" She filled her voice with the awe due the moment.

"Look, there's two more. See if you can reach out and touch them."

The boy lunged for the falling crystals, but thankfully, Ben grabbed his leg in time to keep him from tumbling. Walking Bird's hand waved too much to capture those, but he managed to touch a different one as flakes began falling in steady succession. His squeal flooded her chest with pleasure. And even more so when he threw his head back to allow the snow to pelt his face, sticking out his tongue to capture any that would land there. His giggle filled the air and warmed her all the way through.

This joy was one of the many things she loved about children. Uncomplicated. Their little hearts so open, ready to embrace pleasure.

She looked up at his father, who watched the boy with an expression she couldn't begin to decipher.

Adults remained far harder to understand.

CHAPTER 6

"Shh. Quiet, daughter. We have to be quiet." In the darkness, Goes Ahead paced the opening to the little cave, bouncing and swaying with Pretty Shield as he walked. His words did nothing to dim her frantic crying. With his body so exhausted from the long day caring for his children on horseback, and his mind numb from the list of things they needed—and the worries about everything he didn't know—he had very little left to help his daughter now hours from dawn.

Why did it always seem his daughter and the other babe woke at the same moment? And always hungry, especially in the dark times. Right now, Lola fed her daughter, so he had to quiet his own until her turn came. Had Pretty Shield always eaten so often? He couldn't remember Walking Bird being so hungry as a babe. His daughter had been less than a moon old when he'd left to pursue his son's kidnappers. Those former days seemed like a hazy dream.

Pretty Shield's cries grew louder, if that were possible, spurring helplessness that raced through him. What could he do? He had nothing to give her except a bit of smoked meat or camas cake, but Bright Eyes had insisted babes couldn't eat such until they could sit up. And this tiny daughter was far from managing that feat.

Only milk would quiet her, but she couldn't eat until the other child finished. He'd come to this end of the cave so her fretting wouldn't wake the others, but surely no one could sleep through wails that echoed off the stone walls. He couldn't take her outside, where icy wind swept across the snow-covered mountainside. He'd never imagined how hard it would be to keep a baby warm. For some reason, he'd thought she would be able to bear the cold as a grown woman could.

Or maybe he'd not considered it at all. He knew nothing of children so tiny. Why would the gods think he could keep these two safe until they reached help across the mountains?

He stiffened. No. He would *be* whatever he needed to be and *do* whatever he needed to do to keep his children alive and healthy. He'd watched too many brothers and sisters succumb to injuries and sickness—every one of his siblings, even his brother who'd survived his early days, the one Goes Ahead had thought he'd always have.

He would *not* allow the same to happen to his son and daughter.

Pretty Shield's cries surged again, panic lacing her tone. Desperation filled his own chest. He had to do something to help her.

"Goes Ahead?"

He barely heard the quiet voice over his daughter's sobs, but he spun to face Elise as she stepped from the darkened interior into the moonlight at the cave's opening.

Her wide eyes held concern as she studied him, and her gaze dropped to the babe in his arms, then lifted back to his face. "Can I try to soothe her?" She looked hesitant, as though he might refuse.

He was long past the point of letting distrust keep him from accepting her help. He'd proven far less capable of caring for the children than any other challenge he'd attempted. Elise, though, possessed a remarkable touch with both of them. If anything besides food would quiet his tiny daughter, Elise's gentle soothing could do it.

He held out the bundle, and she reached for her. Even before she brought Pretty Shield close to her body, she murmured in a soothing tone. "There, sweet one." She drew her close and swayed, adding a little bounce.

Pretty Shield's frantic cries eased to a gentler level. Not stopping altogether, but not nearly so desperate. Elise's words shifted to humming as her sway became more pronounced. The sweetness in her tone filled the air around them, and Pretty Shield finally quieted to a few hiccupped sobs. As tired as he was, the beauty in her rhythm might put him to sleep where he stood.

He eased out a long breath, letting his angst slip away with the spent air. Lit by the moonlight like that, the woman and babe made a sight far more pleasing than he ever would have thought. Perhaps it was merely the beauty of his daughter finally satisfied that drew him. Seeing her in so much distress had clenched his insides like a fist.

After a few more moments, Elise stopped humming and looked down on the babe with a sweet smile. Perhaps it was a trick of the shadows, but she seemed to gaze at Pretty Shield with the same love Bright Eyes had—the love of a mother.

Did she have children of her own? If so, they would be with her, surely. Had she lost them? Through death or capture? His body tightened. Perhaps she'd had no control over how they left her care. But he couldn't stomach the weakness of a person who wouldn't fight till her last breath to protect her children.

Yet as she looked up at him, the sweetness in her expression eased the tension inside him. Especially when his gaze slipped down to his daughter's face, finally content now that she slumbered. Her mouth had slackened, her tiny lips parted in complete rest.

Elise laid her cheek on Pretty Shield's head. "She likes to be held upright, not laying back, and with her ear pressed here where she can hear your heartbeat. I think it makes her feel safe to hear that steady thumping."

Safe. This woman made his daughter feel safe. He could learn these skills from her.

He nodded understanding. "What else does she like?"

She tipped her head, as if in thought. Then the corners of her mouth lifted. "To have a full belly, but that's not something either of us can give her."

A painful reminder he didn't need.

Her swaying resumed. "I've seen you rock and bounce with her. She likes that a lot. And to be warm, wrapped tight in her blanket and the thicker fur." Her brows dipped low. "She seems to appreciate very soft things, especially the feel of the rabbit fur when I change her diaper. She might enjoy it if I give her one of the extra rabbit skins to wrap around her beneath her blanket. One of my sisters had a penchant for soft things. She would snuggle them close to her face every time she wanted to sleep."

If a rabbit skin soothed his daughter, he would bring her a hundred of them. He would have to wait until they crossed these mountains though.

Another part of what Elise said gave him pause. "Your sister was much younger?" Perhaps if he knew more of her people and where she'd come from, he would know better whether he could trust her.

Her eyes lit, and her mouth pressed in a smile that seemed to say much. "I have four sisters younger and three brothers, also two older sisters and two older brothers. There are twelve of us in all. My older sisters married early, so I and my next sister down spent much of our time helping with the younger ones.

Babies like Pretty Shield are so much easier than when they grow up enough to tire you out."

Even more tired than he was now? Well...he wasn't ready to think about that now. Walking Bird sprang to mind. Yes, if the lad weren't constrained on horseback all day, he would be even more of a challenge to manage.

He studied her as his sluggish mind again thought through what she'd said. Younger sisters and brothers. Was that how she'd developed such a special way with children? Especially those not her own? Twelve siblings. Such a big family. There must have been deaths. He had to ask. "The others...your brothers and sisters. They lived?"

Her brows drew down. "Yes. There was one babe stillborn, but she's not counted among the twelve. I suppose perhaps she should be included in the number, but she never had the chance to take a breath."

He let out his own air. Twelve children and none lost. It seemed impossible. How much of that was due to this woman standing here before him? "And you...have none of your own?"

Her eyes widened. "Children?" She looked flustered. "Nay. None. I've never been married."

More relief flooded his chest than should have. He shouldn't care that she had no attachment. Only that she'd shown herself capable of both caring for and protecting children, since she was helping with his own.

As long as she spoke the truth. Yet everything he'd seen of her abilities agreed with her words.

Her expression turned curious. "What of you? Do you have family in the village where we're going?"

A weight pressed on his chest. He didn't want to talk about his family. Yet, after her kindness, he shouldn't refuse to answer. "My father and mother. They are growing old, but I think they will welcome us." Though bringing his children into their care was the very last thing he wanted to do. He would have to be on his guard even more. He couldn't let his son and daughter suffer the fate of all the others.

Elise watched him, and it seemed almost as if she could see more than what he showed. "Have they ever met your children?"

He shook his head. "They do not know of them."

She nodded. "I can understand the journey would be too hard to visit them without a strong reason."

It was more than that, though. He didn't want his children—his new life—to be tainted by the pain of those people. If he had any choice now…

She studied him carefully. "You don't want to go there."

Had he lost his ability to hide his thoughts from his expression? Or did she simply see more than others?

He should ignore the question. Refuse to reveal so much. But for some reason, he wanted to tell her. He dropped his gaze to his daughter as he spoke. "I want my children to be safe. To live long lives. I'm not sure they can do so in that place. But I have no other way to care for them if we don't go there."

Her brow gathered low, the shadows deepening lines there. He'd said too much, yet not enough. He would need to tell more. "I, too, had many brothers and sisters. Two sisters and six brothers. None lived more than five winters except Crow Calling. He died after falling from his horse when my father took him on his first buffalo hunt his eleventh summer."

When he stopped speaking, quiet surrounded them, and pain from his words lingered in the air. Smothered out the air actually, for there seemed nothing left to breathe, only the ache of those memories.

"Goes Ahead." The way she whispered his name took away a small bit of the awfulness and replaced it with clean air he could breathe. "I'm so sorry. I can't even imagine how hard that must have been." She paused, and it looked like she wanted to say more, but she hesitated. "You're worried the same will happen to your precious children."

She understood his thoughts fully.

"You said Crow Calling passed away from injury. Was there a sickness that took the others?"

He lifted one shoulder, but the motion didn't feel as casual as he wanted it to. "Not one sickness. Two lived only a few days after birth, one drowned in the river when he was three winters old, two died from injuries, and two others from the spotting sickness. My mother and father both had the spotting sickness, too, yet they survived." He had lived through it also, with only a few scars to show for what they'd lost.

She took a step closer to him, gentling her voice even more than its usual sweet sound. "You think your parents are to blame for so many of their children passing?"

"How can they not be?" He spoke the words too loud, especially with so many sleeping at the other end of the cave. Even after all these years, clearly his anger hadn't waned.

Elise didn't flinch. "I don't know the situations, but I can well imagine how much your mother grieves the loss of her children. Losing even one child is too much, but eight…I'm not sure I could bear it. She must be a strong woman indeed. I'm sure she treasures you and will be overjoyed to have you back, and grandchildren to love. Perhaps she thought she lost you forever too. I think there will be much rejoicing when she meets these precious little ones."

Goes Ahead pressed his eyes shut. Elise had just put into words what he'd not allowed himself to think of. He'd stripped his parents of their last child by leaving as he had. He told them they would never see him again. How much had his mother grieved his loss as well?

He'd watched her after each of the others died. The times she hid herself away. His father's mother would come in and bring food for him and his father and any other children who'd remained, while his mother spent hours, sometimes days, away from their lodge. Then she would return, a quieter version of herself. It would take several moons before she behaved like his mother again.

A weight touched his arm, slight through the thickness of his sleeve. It drew him from the memories, calling him back to the present. As hard as it was to help his children when he knew so little, he would gladly take this trial over those dark days.

He met Elise's gaze, and she stood close enough that he could see her heart in the dark pools of her eyes. Maybe it was that passion that made her beautiful, despite the fact she was a white woman.

The corners of her mouth curved. "Would you like to hold her? Snuggling a babe always lifts my spirit." She started to pull Pretty Shield away from her.

He shook his head and stepped back, dropping her hand from his arm. "She's asleep." The last thing he needed was to awaken her and start those cries again.

Elise's smile curled a little more. "She'll stay asleep, especially when she can hear her papa's heartbeat."

As Elise moved the bundle of blankets and babe from her chest to his, he wrapped his clumsy hands around his daughter. Elise adjusted the position of the bundle, nestling it higher in the curve of his arm. This did feel more comfortable than the way he usually held the babe.

She took his wrist and moved it around so his hand cupped his daughter's head. "There. Now she'll feel safe and loved." Though Elise wore gloves, the feel of her hand on his skin made him far more aware of her than he should be.

When she finally pulled back, his body eased, and he turned his focus to his daughter. She was such a slight thing, and she still slept even after coming to him. As carefully as he could manage, he lowered his head to rest the side of his jaw on top of her blankets. He breathed in the feel of her, though bundled as she was, it might not be her that he was feeling.

Yet this moment felt sacred. At last, he could be with his daughter without fear that he wasn't giving what she needed.

After long minutes, he opened his eyes, and his gaze caught on Elise's. Her eyes shimmered as though she felt the wonder too. He swallowed down the knot clogging his throat, but even still, his voice came out thick. "Thank you." For this moment and so much more.

CHAPTER 7

*G*oes Ahead sat upright in the early morning darkness, moving as slowly as he could to keep from waking his son. The boy had slept all night for the first time since leaving the Sioux, and even Pretty Shield had only awakened to eat twice. Lola must finally have enough to feed both babes as much as they needed. Three sleeps had passed since that night in the cave when Elise taught him how to soothe his daughter. He'd had a great deal of practice since then.

Now, he had to find food for the rest of them. He'd not had enough wits about him to take extra food from their village, there was only what was left from his trip to recapture his son, as well as what the others carried. From what he could tell, they only had another day's worth of food. He'd been hoping to come across a herd of goats or sheep on the mountains while they rode, but none so far.

Last night they'd camped near a small creek, and he'd spotted a trail the animals took to reach the water. If he positioned himself there before the sun brightened the sky, he should gain enough food to last them several days. Maybe more.

As he stood, he cast his gaze over the group sleeping around the fire. Thankfully, much of the snow had melted, and they'd found shelter between a stand of trees and the tall cliff of the mountain. Here, the wind didn't find them often.

Both his son and daughter slept and would likely continue to until he returned. Maybe he should tell Elise his plan, so if one of his children awakened, she could quiet them before they raised the entire group.

But when he stepped closer to her, exhaustion still slackened her features. Her blankets rose and fell with a deep, restful sleep that she likely needed as much as his little ones did.

She always awoke any time either of his children stirred anyway. He could count on her doing the same now.

He adjusted the knife hanging from his neck and secured his tomahawk at his side. As he reached for his bow and quiver, a tiny voice made him pause.

"Father?"

His belly clenched. If Walking Bird awoke fussing, he would go back to sleep. But if he started talking right away, it meant he would be up for the day. Still...

Goes Ahead crouched beside their sleeping pallet and kept his voice to a low whisper. "What is it, my son? The sky is still dark. Go back to sleep."

"Where are you going? I come." His eyes opened fully, wide even, in the darkness. Darkness that wasn't so black anymore. Goes Ahead had to get moving or he wouldn't reach the place he'd planned before the animals came.

It looked like Walking Bird wouldn't fall back to sleep though. Could the boy come with him? "I go to hunt. Can you be as quiet as the deer?"

The boy gave a strong nod.

"Come then." He motioned, and his son scrambled to his feet.

Goes Ahead reached for the small fur Elise had given Walking Bird to use as a cloak. She'd been wise to realize his son needed more to protect him from the cold than the coat growing too small for him. Maybe when they reached Goes Ahead's father's village, his mother would make a new coat for Walking Bird, one that would last him until the warm days. Though with the slow pace they had to travel for the children's sake, the warm days might come before they ever reached that village.

"Ready." Walking Bird spoke a bit too loud.

Goes Ahead pressed a finger to his lips, then motioned his son to follow as they crept out of camp and toward the water.

The rising sun already lit its path as they walked. Walking Bird's tread sounded as loud as a horse stomping through the grass, so Goes Ahead paused his son and pressed his finger to his lips again. Then he motioned to his feet and whispered. "Land on your toe and roll back to your heel so the animals can't hear you coming."

The boy's brow scrunched as he took a step forward, walking only on his toes. "Like this?"

The sight was a little funny but not what Goes Ahead meant. He crouched by his son's foot and cupped it in both hands, then showed the rolling motion that needed to become like breathing to him. He would've thought the boy had already learned it. Wasn't every son born of the People able to walk silently from his first steps?

Maybe not. Guilt struck another blow to Goes Ahead. Had he failed him in this, too, not teaching him the ways of the land?

Once Walking Bird managed several steps as he showed, they resumed their path to the animal crossing. They'd have to creep even quieter than usual in case deer had already come to water.

As they neared the place, Goes Ahead rested a hand on his son's shoulder to slow him, and they moved into a position behind some low saplings. Once his son had taken a position where he could see the water's edge without being clearly seen, Goes Ahead readied an arrow in his bow. They might wait like

59

this for a while, but he would have only one chance when the game arrived.

They settled into quiet, and soon the birds began their morning song. As long as he and his son stayed still, the birdsong would keep the animals that came for water from suspecting a predator waited for them.

Leaves crackled beside him, and he looked down as his son shifted from one foot to the other. His sway knocked him off balance, and the boy reached for one of the small tree branches to catch himself. Of course, the twig snapped from his weight, and around them the birdsong ceased.

Only an ominous silence filled the air.

A flicker of movement through the branches jerked Goes Ahead's gaze up. A deer froze in the distance. Three deer. The first one possessed a small rack of antlers, and the two behind it appeared to be mother and midsized offspring.

The buck sniffed the air, but in the half-breath it took Goes Ahead to sight and draw back his arrow, the animals took flight.

Frustration washed through him, and he lowered the bow but kept his arrow notched.

When he looked down to reprimand his son, the boy lay half-collapsed in the crook of the small tree's branches. His grin flashed wide. Clearly, he had no idea he'd just sent away the food they desperately needed.

How many times had he seen his son smile lately? Only when Elise or her brother played with him. Goes Ahead hadn't worked a grin from him even once these past days. Had he even tried?

Still, he had to teach the lad how serious hunting was. How careful one must be, or the people who depended on them would go hungry. During a hard winter, losing prey like those deer could mean their entire group died of starvation.

His belly clenched, though not from hunger. With his last breath he would make sure his children never met such a fate.

His son's gaze moved from him to something behind him, and the boy's eyes rounded.

Goes Ahead spun, drawing back the arrow and bowstring again. A heartbeat passed before he found what had drawn Walking Bird's attention. Crouched on the limb above them, a long tawny body stretched out, its tail creeping through the air in a measured cadence.

Wildcat.

Its gaze locked on them, its muscles coiled tight.

Goes Ahead's body reacted before his mind could catch up, raising the bow and drawing tighter on the arrow. With a smooth release, he sent the arrow through the short distance, plunging exactly where he'd aimed in the animal's side.

An angry screech broke the morning's quiet as the cat jerked with the force of the blow. Its body tipped sideways off the limb even as it scrambled to stay on its perch. A gasp slipped from it, meaning his arrow's tip had punctured a lung.

Death would be sure now. Not only would they have meat to sustain them another day, but Goes Ahead had protected his son from one of the worst of predators.

~

"How are you holding up, my friend?" Elise studied Lola as they rode in the slight warmth of the early afternoon sun. They'd had their hands full with the children these past five days on the trail, so the two of them hadn't had time for the long conversations she'd come to love.

Even now, Lola nursed little Anna while she rode. She looked up from her daughter and offered Elise a weary smile. "I'm well. Glad I finally have enough milk to give these two a full meal when they're hungry."

"I'm relieved for your sake and theirs. You desperately need a full night's sleep." The shadows under Lola's eyes looked far too much like bruises.

Lola's eyelids drooped halfway. "I can't even remember what sleeping through a night feels like." Then her gaze shifted to Pretty Shield, who lay nestled in the sling across Elise's chest. Goes Ahead had become much more comfortable allowing her to take one of the children. Her heart would never grow tired of snuggling this sweet bundle, though her back might disagree.

"I'm just glad I can help." The weariness slipped away from Lola's expression as she smiled at Pretty Shield. Then her gaze lifted to Elise. "You were right in what you said when we first met him. This is the way I can be hands and feet to Goes Ahead and his sweet daughter."

For some reason, a knot of emotion clogged Elise's throat. "You're able to do far more than the rest of us. I'm just glad he's allowing us to help. It seems like he trusts us a little more now." She wrapped a hand around the sling to cradle the babe. "I'm trying not to do anything to break that trust."

Lola raised her brows. "You're helping them night and day, loving his children as though they're your own. Without you, he'd be exhausted and overwhelmed." Her friend narrowed her eyes, perhaps looking deeper than she should. "Besides, what could you do to break his trust? How could he possibly not adore you? You're so kind and such a wonderful example of God's love, even without all you're doing."

Warmth crept up Elise's neck, and she shifted her gaze forward. Not so much from embarrassment, but... She shrugged. "Doing things for people always helps gain their good opinion."

"And you want him to like you." Though Lola's voice was gentle, she didn't speak the words as a question but a statement of fact.

Again, Elise shrugged, keeping her gaze ahead. Who didn't

want to be liked by others? There was nothing special about this man except the fact that he was harder to win over than most.

"There's something you don't realize, Elise. You don't have to *do* anything to make him or anyone else like you. You're special just as you are, full of joy and lovely to be around. The things you do are appreciated, but it's your personality, the essence of you, that people are drawn to."

For some reason Elise's silly throat clogged again. She could think of nothing to respond with. Lola's words were a reflection of her kind heart, and definitely an exaggeration about Elise.

But her friend spoke again. "And don't try to deflect what I said by nonsense about me just being kind. You know I'm not one to speak something unless it's true."

A smile tickled Elise's mouth, and she looked over at her friend. "Like when you told Anna she was the prettiest baby ever born?"

Lola's brows drew low, and she flicked her gaze down to Pretty Shield, giving a mock frown. "Hush. Do I need to restate the part about being kind? Don't say things like that around others who might be wounded by it."

As if she understood, Pretty Shield began to squirm in her sling, letting out a fussing noise.

Lola's voice took on the singing tone she used with the babes. "Of course, other than Anna, Pretty Shield is the prettiest little girl I've ever seen. Such a sweetness about her."

Elise chuckled as she raised the babe into a position where she could better soothe her. "I certainly agree there," she said to the child. "Mrs. Lola might be biased, but I'm not."

As Elise stared into those sweet trusting eyes, she ignored the snort from her friend. She might be a little partial, but no one could help falling in love with this precious babe.

CHAPTER 8

The ominous clouds shadowing the horizon grew thicker the farther they road. Elise eyed them, and her muscles tensed. These didn't have the same low pressing weight the snow clouds had. They appeared more rounded and a darker charcoal with a little navy mixed in to give them a bruised look. But they certainly portended rain...maybe worse.

Conditions their little group didn't need while scaling the treacherous rocks on this mountain slope. As far as she could tell, the peak they climbed now was the tallest they'd attempted yet, and they'd just crested the ridge, which meant they still had close to a full day's ride to the bottom on the far side.

What's more, this slope provided almost no trees for shelter, only a few scraggly bush-like saplings that managed to cling to the rocky ground.

She glanced at her brother, who rode with Walking Bird sleeping against his back. "Will it just be rain?"

He met her look with a grim set to his mouth. "That's what I'd say, but White Owl or Goes Ahead may know better." He glanced back at White Owl.

Their friend nodded. "Rain, yes, and light flashes. We should make cover."

Make cover with what? As she turned forward again to look for a place where they could construct something, Goes Ahead pointed down the slope. "That cliff, and trees to tie furs over us."

He spoke as though he'd already been forming a plan. And the place where he pointed looked like it might be the best option.

As the horses picked their way to the spot, a low rumble sounded in the distance. White Owl was right. By the time they halted, large raindrops splattered on them and thunder had sounded twice more.

She slid to the ground and took Pretty Shield from Goes Ahead, then with her other hand, she eased Walking Bird down from behind Ben's saddle. She couldn't hold him with the babe in her arms, but she crouched down to help him awaken gently. "Hello there, sweet boy. It's time to wake up and make camp."

The boy rubbed sleepy eyes, but when thunder growled a bit louder, those eyes popped wide.

"It's all right. Just a bit of rain and thunder. Your Papa's going to put up a cover for us."

The men quickly pulled out the extra furs and tied them together to form a low canopy with the cliff wall on one side. She and Lola removed the packs they would need from the saddles and gathered the children under the deepest part of the covering, where the rain running down the mountainside shouldn't reach them. Walking Bird clung to her arm as he stared wide-eyed into the weather outside their shelter. It must have unnerved him to be awakened into such chaos.

Drops now fell in earnest, soaking the horses and the men as they worked to strip saddles and secure the animals.

There was still so much to do to make camp, including gather wood—what little kindling they could find on this mountainside—before it became fully soaked.

Elise rose to her knees and leaned close enough to Lola to be heard over the patter of rain. "Can the children stay with you while I gather firewood?"

"No!" Walking Bird clutched her arm tighter, nearly pulling her back down in his panic.

She turned to the boy and tried to extract herself from his grasp so she could wrap her arm around him. Her other hand was full holding Pretty Shield.

But he wouldn't release her, terror marking his expression. She pulled her arm closer to her side, drawing him in as she sat back down. "It's all right, honey. You're safe. There's nothing to fear."

When she made a place for him, the boy nearly dove into her lap. Another clap of thunder sounded much nearer than the others, and a sob shuddered through his body.

She wrapped her arm tight around him, rocking side to side as she cradled him and his sister together. "It's all right. I love you. God loves you. He's watching over us. We have nothing to fear." She murmured those same words over and over, and when a flash of lightning and nearby thunder rumbled, she added one of her favorite verses for courage. "Greater is He that is in you than he that is in the world."

By the time the men finished with the animals and ducked back under the shelter with loads of wood, water dripping from their coats, lightning and thunder flashed and crashed in quick succession. Walking Bird no longer quivered with each blast, but he still curled tightly against her body.

Goes Ahead's gaze met hers as he strode to her. The covering hung too low for him to stand upright, so he stripped off his wet coat, then dropped to his knees and scooped his son into his arms, then settled into a sitting position. The boy perched in the crook of his father's arm and leaned over to wrap his little hands around Goes Ahead's neck, laying his head on the broad shoulder.

He spoke to his son in their language, giving the boy a little bounce. She couldn't tell if Walking Bird answered or not with his face pressed against his father and the clamor of the storm around them.

White Owl had gone to his wife, and the two spoke quietly as he dug through one of their packs. Thankfully, Ben started a fire from the dry wood they carried for an occasion such as this. The men must be nearly frozen from being drenched in the frigid winter air.

Goes Ahead spoke to his son again, and the boy pulled back enough to see his father's face, though he stayed close. Whatever he asked, Goes Ahead nodded agreement to. But when Walking Bird spoke again, Goes Ahead's nose scrunched in an almost comical frown. She'd never seen him so animated. Then he nodded a begrudging acquiescence.

Walking Bird scrambled to turn around in his father's lap so his back pressed against Goes Ahead's strong chest, his head resting in the crook of his father's neck.

Goes Ahead looked up at her, his gaze a little sheepish. He started to speak, but another clap of thunder interrupted him. Walking Bird didn't jump this time, cradled as he was in the strength of his father's arms. When the sound died away, Goes Ahead began again. "He wishes me to tell him a story, but in English so the little ones can understand." He nodded toward Anna. If a babe so young could comprehend, she would already be accustomed to their language.

Warmth swept through Elise. He would do this thing that might be considered trivial to many men, telling a child a story. In English so they could all understand, which might embarrass him. All because his son asked, and probably to help distract him from his fears of the storm.

She motioned to the rock wall beside her. "You'll be more comfortable with something to lean against." He'd be more comfortable in dry clothes, too, but he might not have a second set. And she wasn't ready to discuss his clothing. He was a grown man after all. If he wanted to change, well...

There wasn't really a place that allowed privacy here. He didn't shiver that she could tell, so perhaps the fire would be enough to warm him.

He did as she suggested, scooting back against the rock. When he settled in, only a handsbreadth separated her arm from his. His warmth seeped through her coat, even though they didn't touch. This man wouldn't freeze to death anytime soon. Or perhaps it was only her awareness of him that heated her so.

His voice rumbled low and deep, easily carrying over the steady rain falling outside their shelter. "There was a boy about your age, or maybe one winter older. He had a brother who taught him many things. How to draw a bow and select the best branches for arrows. How to know the difference between the tracks of the wolf and those of the coyote. How to hear when animals say the winter will be cold or warm. The brother was older—six winters older. And the little boy admired him very much. They had only one horse to ride, and they rode together far, day after day. They brought rabbit meat to their mother, and skins for the little ones." His gaze flicked to Pretty Shield in her arms, but it wasn't pleasure that touched his eyes when he looked at his daughter. Only sadness.

Was he remembering the siblings who'd died so young? The boys in his story must be him and his older brother, the one who died in the buffalo hunt at age eleven. Before, when he'd spoken of his brother, she'd thought they must have played together. But she'd never imagined all the happy days in this story. Were they real or wishful imaginings?

Walking Bird's little voice barely rose above the rain. "I can bring rabbit skins for the babies. From our pack."

His father nodded. "But soon, you will hunt rabbit and bring fresh skins to be dried and scraped. You can bring more rabbit skin to replace the old."

The lad looked up at his father, and Goes Ahead dipped his chin to meet his son's gaze. Walking Bird's boyish voice sounded so serious. "You show me how? I hunt with you?"

"Yes." Goes Ahead nodded.

Walking Bird turned to his sister, who'd settled into a deep sleep in Elise's arms. He pressed a hand on the babe's blanket. "You hear, Shield? I bring new fur to you."

His sweetness nearly melted Elise's heart completely, and when the boy looked up at her, perhaps seeking confirmation, she nodded. "She would like that. When you're bigger, you and your Papa can bring her new furs." She couldn't help reaching out to stroke the wisps of hair away from his cheeks.

"There." Ben leaned back from the fire and brushed wood dust off his hands. "The fire didn't want to catch with the air so damp, but I think that flame will last." Was he speaking loudly enough to interrupt the sweet exchange on purpose?

Surely Ben didn't mind her nurturing these children, both in body and spirit. Did he fear an affection was growing between her and their father? The thought was ridiculous.

She'd come to show God's love to these people, but nothing more would develop. She might *admire* Goes Ahead. He was turning out to be far different from what she'd assumed when Bright Eyes called him the greatest of warriors. Different from the man she'd thought he was when they first met, staring out over the massacred village. Though he certainly possessed strength of body and capability in this wild country where he lived, his love for his children clearly ran deep. His insecurity about what he didn't know for their care made him all the more appealing.

Again, Ben's words broke through the tender moment, though this time it was only her thoughts he interrupted. "Shall I take the babe, Elise, while you pull out the food? You might like a break from holding her for so long." There was a hint of censure in his tone.

She should pull him aside when they could find a private moment and set him straight. For now though, they would all be better for a meal. Especially her ornery brother.

She nodded. "I don't mind having her with me, but you can hold her for a few minutes if you make sure you don't wake her." As she lifted the sling over her head and passed the sleeping babe to her brother, she had to work not to give him a pointed look.

Or thump him on the head.

She quickly warmed meat and added in a bit of camas cake. It had taken her and Ben a while to adjust to the taste of that particular root—and its impact on her gut—but without the camas so popular with the Flathead tribes, the only thing she and her brother would have eaten last winter would have been smoked salmon. One grew tired of fish for every meal after the first month or so. In the summer, they'd had berries and a variety of other plants. But now, they were down to camas cake and the rest of the wildcat Goes Ahead had killed the other day.

As she laid the food in front of the others, she was careful not to direct her words to anyone in particular. "We have about one more day's worth of meat left, though there is still more camas root."

"Tracks from the mountain goats at top." Goes Ahead pointed toward the peak they'd crested that day. "Maybe hunt them after rain."

She nodded. "We saw a great many goat and sheep herds when Ben and I crossed the mountains last year. But that was farther south of this place, and late summer, before the cold months."

After she cut Walking Bird's meat into smaller bites, she took up her own portion, and silence fell over their group except for the sounds of eating.

Lola finished first, likely because she'd learned to scarf down her food with the baby always needing her. "I suppose we'll be sleeping here then and set out in the morning?"

Elise glanced outside the shelter. The dark clouds made the time feel much later than it probably was—maybe only late afternoon. But the rain showed no sign of letting up. "Surely when we wake tomorrow, the sky will have cleared."

Her gaze moved to Goes Ahead. He didn't act as though the delay concerned him overmuch. They'd surely been traveling slower than he was accustomed to on his own, but a faster pace would be harder for the children.

He didn't meet her look, only stared out at the weather. "See what comes with sun. Rain freeze to ice, make trail slippery. We wait to see."

Her middle tightened. So they might be delayed even longer than this afternoon. As thankful as she was for this shelter, she couldn't help but wonder how small it would become by morning.

CHAPTER 9

*G*oes Ahead tensed as his body came awake. Something pressed against him, something heavier than his son. Walking Bird liked to sleep close, and the boy now rested against Goes Ahead's leg. So what lay on his shoulder?

Thoughts flashed through his mind like lightning. He was sleeping upright, hard stone at his back. Which meant they were under the shelter, keeping warm from the rain.

And the weight on his shoulder? He eased an eyelid open, not allowing himself even to breathe. Elise had moved beside him to take Pretty Shield sometime in the night. The last time he looked at her, she'd been sleeping with her head on her brother's arm. His daughter had finally slept nestled in her lap, wrapped tightly in furs.

His gaze found Pretty Shield first, still in that same position, Elise's hand resting on her, either to comfort or protect. Elise had become like a mother to his children.

Bright Eyes should be here, nursing their babe and soothing their son through the storm. It wasn't right that her life had been snuffed out. What would she think of Elise—a white woman, though he rarely thought of her that way anymore—tending her son and daughter in her stead?

She would be thankful they were loved and cared for.

He knew that without a doubt, though its reality clogged his throat. She'd been such a good mother and wife, far better than he'd been as a husband to her. He'd never given her the time and attention she wanted from him—he simply hadn't known how. Their marriage had started out as a trade match, and when she'd wanted more from him... Well, he'd never been able to satisfy the hope in her eyes when she looked at him.

But as his gaze tracked up his arm and settled on the pale forehead framed by loose hair draping either side, his heart picked up speed.

Why did this woman affect him so? She was everything he disliked. Everything he distrusted. Yet her goodness set her apart. The way she loved his children had broken down his defenses. The way she was always at his side, like a partner, though that was the last thing he'd wanted. She carried the weight of his responsibilities when he couldn't manage another moment.

And now, feeling her warmth against him. Seeing her beauty. From this position just above her, he couldn't miss the length of her lashes, the perfect roundness of her cheeks, how straight her nose, and the curve of her lips. His body warmed far too much at the thought of tasting those lips.

He shouldn't let himself think such things. She probably felt nothing for him. And he would never take even a taste if she weren't agreeable.

He should rise and move away. Break the hold she was claiming over him with her nearness.

But if he did so, not only would he awaken her, but likely also his children. And if there was one truth he'd learned these past sleeps, it was that, when the little ones finally succumbed to rest, he should do everything possible to keep them that way.

Even if it required him to stay with the warmth of this woman pressed against him.

As he studied her expression, watched the rise and fall of her breathing, he had a feeling she might have so fully woven herself into his heart without him realizing it that neither he nor his children would ever be the same.

∽

"*I*'m sorry, little one. I know it's cold." Elise hurried to wipe away the soiled grass from Pretty Shield's diaper and tuck clean material into the rabbit skin. Both days since the thunderstorm, the temperature had dropped lower than the day before. Now she could barely stand to remove her gloves while she changed diapers. How much harder it must be for the babes to have their bottoms exposed for the task.

"I'm going to ready our horses." Ben hoisted one saddle over each of his shoulders and stooped to hold them both in place while he walked. White Owl and Goes Ahead had already gone to do the same while she and Lola finished preparing the children and Ben packed the last of the camp supplies. They needed to get on the trail soon.

Her brother paused to wink at Walking Bird where the boy sat playing with his blocks. "Maybe we'll see more drawings on the rocks today."

The lad's face lit at the reminder of their discovery yesterday. Apparently, past travelers through this area had carved a story from their journey on one of the cliff walls. Walking Bird had enjoyed Ben's dramatic retelling—using his imagination to fill in some of the details.

As Ben continued down the slope, she glanced at his retreating back. "Tell Goes Ahead I found a bundle of dried grass so he doesn't need to pick more yet." They wouldn't have a way to adequately dry it as they traveled, especially not with this icy wind whipping so fiercely across the mountainside.

Her brother bobbed his head to show he'd heard but didn't turn around. Ben had seemed a little strange toward Goes Ahead these past few days, as though he was uncertain about the man. She'd felt the same when they first began traveling together, but the more she saw him—especially around his children—and the more she learned through talking with him, the stronger her conviction grew that not only did they not need to worry about their safety with him, but he was truly a good man. Now if he would only open himself to receive the love God longed to shower on him.

Then maybe she wouldn't have to guard her own heart so tightly.

Before that longing could consume her thoughts, Lola spoke from where she nursed her daughter. "It seems like Goes Ahead listens quite closely to our morning devotions. Do you think some of God's word is taking hold?"

Her pulse gave a little flurry at the thought. "I hope so." She usually spent the time during Ben's Bible readings trying *not* to look at Goes Ahead.

Lord, touch his heart. Make him eager for the truth of Your love. And help me not to want it only for selfish reasons.

After tucking Pretty Shield's blankets around her, Elise lifted the babe to her shoulder and stood, then reached for the bundle of the child's supplies. "I'm going to go see how I can help with the horses."

She started to call out to Walking Bird to gather his blocks so he could accompany her, but Lola waved her down. "He's playing so nicely. I'll bring him when I finish feeding Anna."

She glanced from her friend's confident expression to where the boy was, indeed, enjoying the quiet play by himself. A rarity for the active lad. "If you're sure."

"Of course. Let him have a few more minutes with his toys."

Elise started down the slope toward the level area where they'd hobbled the horses to eat overnight. As she drew near, the sound of men's voices drifted through the shrubby trees separating her from the animals.

Ben sounded almost angry. She slowed to make out his words.

"You can't push women and children so hard. They're just babies. They could die from a simple cold. And how could they not take sick after so many hours in this harsh wind?"

Her heart beat faster. Why was Ben saying that? He knew they were doing everything possible to protect the babies, and Walking Bird too. They simply had to get through these mountains to reach better conditions.

As she increased her pace to a quick step to reach the men and cease her brother's ranting, Goes Ahead's spoke. She slowed again to hear him, but his voice came quieter than her brother's, so she had to hold her breath to make out most of his words.

"…know dangers.…must get through. … snow again this day. If you think…too much…stop. The journey hard… not lose anyone. Especially not my children." His voice rose with those last words, making it easier to hear. He stated them almost like a declaration. And no wonder, after what he'd shared about his siblings.

She started forward again, making her footsteps as loud as she could—not a hard task as her feet loosened pebbles, sending them skittering down the slope.

Thankfully, the men quieted. When she reached them, Ben focused on saddling his mare and had already finished with her gelding.

White Owl worked with a pack behind his saddle.

Goes Ahead stood at his stallion's head, watching her as she approached. He must be wondering why she didn't bring his son as she'd said she would.

"Walking Bird was playing with his blocks. Lola said she would bring him down when she comes."

A frown touched his brow. "I will go get him."

Elise tried not to let his words frustrate her. After all, he was probably on edge from the dressing down Ben just gave him.

As Goes Ahead secured his horse to a tree, White Owl stepped away from his mare. "I will help my wife."

As the men filed past her, she didn't miss the glance White Owl sent Goes Ahead. It wasn't unkind, but a bit of wariness lived there. Did he worry about the man being alone with his wife and daughter? Surely he realized by now he had no need for that concern.

A new thought slipped in, one she hadn't considered before. What history lay between their tribes? Why hadn't she thought to ask that question? She'd learned so much about the Shoshone, the Nez Perce, and the Salish whom she and Ben had lived among, and even the Blackfoot they'd met on occasion.

But except for that one short meal with the Gros Ventre tribe when they first arrived in this country, she knew little about them. And nothing about whether the Gros Ventre were friendly with the Shoshone, White Owl's people.

That would have to be a question for later. This might be her only chance to talk to Ben alone.

She walked up beside him and stroked his mare's neck, keeping her voice low as she spoke. "I heard what you were saying to Goes Ahead." She paused to allow time for a response from him. Anything to gauge his mood.

His tone came out terse. "Thought you might have." Still angry then. Was it only the cold weather that had her easygoing brother so riled? There must be something more.

She would tread carefully, but she had to encourage him to be more careful of his words. "I know the cold and the long days in the saddle are hard, but I don't think Goes Ahead is pushing us more than we can handle. We're all taking extra care to protect the little ones from the weather. We simply have to get through these mountains. All will be better on the other side."

She took a breath and added the most important part in a gentler tone. "We should all be careful how we speak to Goes Ahead. He knows of our faith, and we are God's voice to him."

Ben glared at her. "I understand that. I'm trying to be careful, but it's hard not to be frustrated with the position he's putting you and Lola and the children in."

Urgency welled in her chest. How could she make him see? "We're doing fine, Benji. Don't worry about us. Showing God's love to Goes Ahead is far more important than our comfort."

He spun to face her fully, his eyes flashing. "I won't be so focused on winning his soul to the Lord that I let the rest of you die in the process."

His anger nearly made her step back. This had to be from more than just the challenges of the cold.

But then his words slowly took shape in her mind. Goes Ahead's soul? It was of far greater value than their temporary lives here on earth. When they passed on from this place, they would spend eternity with the Lord. But Goes Ahead... She couldn't let herself dwell on what would happen to him if they didn't reach him with the message of God's love.

Ben's face blanched as though he too realized the import of what he'd said. His mouth pressed in a thin line, clearly torn between taking back his words and standing by them. Her heart ached for this brother who had set aside his own plans to accompany her on this missionary journey. He worked so hard to protect her, but sometimes protection wasn't the most important consideration.

She took a step toward him and wrapped her arms around his waist as she hadn't done in so long. For a long moment, she let herself relish the warm protection of her brother's hug.

Soon, she would need to be strong again. For all of them.

CHAPTER 10

*W*hy did Ben's face appear so sour? Goes Ahead's middle churned. He must have done something to draw the ire of Elise's brother, but he knew not what. The frustration about the weather Ben spoke of yesterday morning seemed only a part.

Sometimes the man looked at him with distrust, as though Goes Ahead had painted himself with warpaint, but other times a sadness cloaked Ben's expression.

Goes Ahead guided his stallion along the game trail that led up the side of the mountain. If only they could find game, but no animals had come through here since the last snowfall. He had to focus on keeping the group on the best track through these mountains and making sure his children had everything they needed to stay warm and safe.

And keep all of them well fed.

That last point moved to the forefront as he spotted mountain goat tracks in the snow ahead. They were fresh enough to have been left today.

He lifted his gaze to the top of the peak they were climbing. The tracks led that direction, so they might find a herd yet. The group behind him had been quiet most of the afternoon, especially now since the wind gusted harder the farther up they climbed. Probably no need to tell them not to speak lest the animals hear them and run away.

As they rode upward, something small and dark in the snow caught his gaze. Droppings from the goat herd. And still warm, judging from the steam rising. They were close.

He raised a hand for the group to halt, then turned and spoke softly. "Herd of mountain goats ahead. I go on foot to hunt."

"Should White Owl and I come too?" Ben nudged his mount forward.

"Bring rifles." Goes Ahead slid from his horse without dislodging his son from the stallion's back. A movement he'd perfected.

He'd rather leave the horse here, and he could tie him, but not with Walking Bird sitting alone up there.

When he glanced back at the group, Elise snagged his gaze. "Walking Bird can sit with me while we wait for you."

She already had his daughter in a sling around her front. How much more could he ask of this woman?

But she smiled and patted just behind her saddle. "Right here on my bed roll is perfect for him."

The other two men had already dismounted and readied their rifles and shot bags. So he hoisted his son into the air, giving him an extra lift that won him a smile, before landing the boy in the place Elise had indicated. He pressed his hand to Walking Bird's knee. "Sit quietly." Not an easy feat for his energetic son.

Just before stepping back, Goes Ahead's gaze slipped to Elise's. A sweet smile lit her face. Her beauty caught him every time. If she felt even a little of what he was experiencing, he'd be in real trouble. But she wouldn't look twice at a man of the People like him, not a white woman.

He pulled himself away, then turned and freed his bow and quiver from their straps. Ben and White Owl waited for him to go first, so he started up the slope, following the tracks. There must be at least ten animals, maybe fifteen. He and the other men would likely only get three goats, unless he could bring down a second before the gunfire scattered them.

As he suspected, they found the herd not much farther up. Goes Ahead shot first, bringing down the ram. He planted a second arrow in the center of the herd just as the rifles rang out, sending the animals scattering.

Four to clean and skin. Enough meat to last until they reached the grassland, where the buffalo would be plenty.

As he started forward to begin preparing the animals to skin, Ben held back. "I'll go get the others and bring them up here."

Goes Ahead should've thought of that. He nodded, then turned his focus to the goats. Maybe he could have most of the bleeding done by the time the women and children came.

He didn't linger over the flowing blood—he never did—but even the flash of it brought him back to the red that had smeared Bright Eyes's face. Pain seared through him. He'd not been there when she needed him, hadn't protected those in his care—not her anyway.

He only had his children left. They were his last two chances to prove he could do better than his parents had.

White Owl began cutting the meat out of one of the goats, so Goes Ahead moved to where two had fallen behind a cluster of rocks and started the same task. They should scrape the hides too, but that would require staying on this mountainside the rest of the day. The wind was stronger up here. Would Ben say Goes Ahead was putting the women and children in danger by keeping them in this place the extra time?

He plunged the knife a little harder than he needed to, but the release gave him an outlet for his frustration. It didn't matter what Ben Lane thought. Goes Ahead knew this land

81

better than any of them. He would get them through without losing any of the group.

With quick strokes, he sliced out meat, forcing his attention on the job instead of all the worries that tried to press in.

"Goes Ahead."

He nearly jumped at Elise's voice behind him, and he spun to face her. From the place he worked, the rocks hid him from the others. How had he missed hearing her, even focused on the goat as he was?

She stood with a hunting knife in her hand, her gaze uncertain. "Lola's feeding Pretty Shield, and Anna is watching Walking Bird play with blocks. Ben is helping White Owl, so I thought to come work with you. Can you tell me what to do? I've never field-dressed a mountain goat before. Is it the same as a hog or cow?"

The sight of her—so delicate—wielding that blade. And the way her hands, and likely the rest of her, would be covered in blood by the end of the task... A battle roared in his chest. "I do not know hog or cow, but this is not for you. I will bring the meat. We will find camp not so cold to cook." Her brother was right that the women and children needed protection. The sight of her now cleared any uncertainty from his mind. She was too delicate. He had to safeguard her as much as his tiny daughter and son.

But she straightened, her chin coming up as her eyes flashed. Her hair whipped in the wind, only adding to the stubbornness in her expression. And to her beauty. "I've done this work hundreds of times. I only asked in case there was something different about these goats, but probably not."

She marched toward the second carcass. The one he'd bled but hadn't begun cutting the meat from. He should've known she would not be stopped once she set her mind to help.

She knelt by the animal and began working, showing that,

indeed, she had completed this task many times before. Bright Eyes had too, of course. But this woman seemed so unlike his wife. Simply because she came from a different people? Maybe because her features were finer, more delicate. Yet she had a passion, a determination he'd never seen in Bright Eyes. Something within him connected with Elise Lane in a way he'd never felt connected to the woman who had been his wife. His chest ached, but more from the pain he *should* feel than from what he actually did.

Bright Eyes had been such a good woman. Such a good mother. Her life had been stripped away far too soon. He'd failed her. Failed to protect his own. That part was the hardest to bear.

Maybe this anger surging inside him toward the Sioux should be directed toward himself alone. He'd not left her as protected as he'd thought, there in the village that hadn't seen fighting once during the five years he lived there with her.

"Goes Ahead?" Elise's voice broke into his awareness just as her hand touched his arm.

He whirled but caught himself before striking out. If he hurt her because he was distracted, he wouldn't be able to stand it. How had she managed to approach a second time without him hearing?

"Are you all right?" Her voice sounded so tentative, and worry clouded her face. Concern for him. As if he was worthy enough for her to fret over.

He turned back to the goat with a single nod. But as he surveyed what he'd done so far, his stomach clenched. He'd nearly mutilated the carcass, cutting out more than he should have in some areas and leaving good meat behind in others. He'd even pierced the gut, something his mother had never liked him to do. And the hide, as much as he'd sliced it, would be good for nothing but braiding into rope.

Another surge of anger swept through him, pointed once

more toward himself. Even this simple task he'd ruined by not staying focused.

He'd sprayed blood everywhere, too, the crimson leaking out onto the snow-covered ground, spattering his buckskins, smearing much of his knife and hands. He'd never felt so dirty while carrying out this task. Hunting was good, providing food for his family and those he was responsible for. But *he* was not good.

"What is it? What's wrong?" Her hand still rested on his arm, her voice so sweet with its concern. Too sweet. Too kind.

He stared down into his open hands, his bloody hands, the red-smeared handle of his hunting knife lying in his palm.

What was *wrong*? Everything. He said the only thing he could bring himself to voice aloud. "I'm dirty."

"We can clean you. Here's some snow to use." As she reached for a handful of fresh icy crystals, then ran them over his blood-smeared skin, the words Ben spoke the other morning slipped through his mind.

Though your sins be as scarlet, they shall be as white as snow. Ben had said everyone sinned, doing things they should not. Did that include things he'd not done well enough? Could this God of the white people, this Creator and Father, make him the person he should have been? Could He take away the stain of the blood on his hands, the people he should have saved?

He pulled away from Elise's scrubbing, and when she looked up at him with a question in her eyes, he locked his gaze with hers. "Can your God make me better?"

Her head tilted to the side as she studied him. Perhaps she understood, for she answered. "When we ask God to save us from the punishment we deserve for the wrong things we've done, He takes them away. He gives His Spirit to help us, to live inside us and be our strength so we don't do those wrong things anymore. He helps us do good."

Yes. He gripped her arm. "That is what I want. To not do the

84

wrong things. To do good." For his children. To do whatever it took for their good.

A smile more beautiful than any he'd seen softened her face. "That's wonderful. All you have to do is pray to Him and ask Him to forgive the wrong things and come into your heart. To be the strength inside you to help you do what He wills."

He could pray. His mother had taught him to pray to the sun, though he'd not done so since leaving his father's village.

She shifted her wrist, and his fingers slid down so she could take his hand in hers. All the blood had been cleaned away. "We close our eyes to honor God when we speak with Him."

As she dipped her chin and closed her eyes, he did the same, doing his best not to let the warmth of her skin distract him. This great God deserved his full focus.

The words Elise gave him to say seemed too simple. Yet as he spoke them, a weight seemed to lift from his chest. He'd never felt changed when he'd prayed as a boy, and maybe that word was too strong for this feeling now. Yet his spirit felt...lighter.

When he spoke "amen" after she did, she squeezed his hand. He looked up to meet her gaze, her eyes sparkled, and her smile was impossibly wide.

"The word *amen* means *so be it*, asking God to carry out what we prayed for. And now He's done just that. He's cleared away your sins—the wrong things you've done in your life. He's cleaned them away just like the snow wipes away the blood from your hands, except there's no sign left of your wrongs at all. He's made you a new man, giving you a fresh start. His Spirit is inside you, teaching you the right ways and helping you do those good things. He teaches you what to do in His word, the Bible that Ben reads us each morning."

She squeezed his hand again. "Goes Ahead, I can't tell you how happy this makes me. The Bible says all who follow God become His children, brothers and sisters with Him as our Father."

Something flashed in her eyes with those last words, like a quick slipping of her smile. Did she not want to be his sister... because he was from the White Clay People? His own spirit gave a far different reason, though surely she didn't feel that way too.

A new awareness had settled between them, a tension that stirred something in his chest. Something that felt a great deal like desire.

She still held his hand, and her warmth became impossible to ignore now. Her fingers shifted within his. Pulling away?

But she didn't pull away, only settled her grasp more firmly within his own. And then her thumb, with the lightest touch, stroked across the back of his hand.

A shot of fire slipped all the way through him. Could she possibly feel any attraction toward him? It seemed so unlikely, yet she held his gaze, her own unwavering...not backing down from the intensity between them.

Slowly, he shifted his hand around hers to be more intentional, giving her little doubt of what he meant by the touch.

Her gaze stayed locked with his, so he reached his other hand up to her neck, sliding his fingers to the base of her hair.

So soft. The strands felt like the finest rabbit fur, and he wove his fingers through.

Her eyelids dipped for a single heartbeat, as though she relished his touch.

Relished. Didn't dread. The thought gave him courage to lean in.

CHAPTER 11

*G*oes Ahead could barely breathe as he let his eyes roam Elise's face. Maybe he pulled her closer with his hand at her neck, or maybe she came of her own accord. But she met him partway, halting with her lips a handsbreadth from his own. Her gaze had dipped to his mouth, lowering her eyelids so their length stood out against the beauty of her skin. Skin not dark at birth, but the sun had tanned her cheeks to a shade nearly the same as many of his people.

But then she lifted her focus to him, catching him with those wide blue eyes, both vulnerable and sure. Had she ever kissed a man? Did she really want this now?

He should pull back. Begin doing those good things God's spirit inside him would give him the strength for.

Before he could draw himself away, Elise closed the distance between them. Her mouth met his with a warm touch, completely untrained. But it sent heat all the way through him. He held himself as still as he could manage, responding only gently to her kiss. This woman was so delicate, she deserved the tenderest of touches.

Though his fingers still wove through her hair, he kept his

hand from sliding farther, instead cradling her head, treasuring her mouth with his. Her innocence made him want to protect her all the more, even from himself.

Especially from himself.

He let her guide the kiss, giving only as much as she wanted to take. And when she pulled back, he didn't draw her close again, as much as his body wanted to.

She moved only far enough for them to see each other, and the sight of her, breathless, her eyes a bit dazed, her lips swollen and red as berries, sent warmth through his chest. She blinked, maybe trying to come out of the haze.

He had no desire to leave this pocket of goodness he'd somehow stepped into. The newness of committing to her God —now his God—then the even greater surprise of Elise's kiss. It still seemed too much to believe that both God *and* Elise would accept him so completely, and that she might see something in him she liked.

At last, she seemed to be coming back to herself. As she did, pink crept over her cheeks, and she dropped her gaze from his. Perhaps this was only the shyness of a maiden. Yet a desperation surged inside him. He searched for something to say, something to pull her out. To make her hold his gaze—to look at him as strongly as she had moments before.

To not regret that kiss.

He worked to force words past his throat. "I did not expect that."

She jerked her gaze up, searching his face. Had he said something wrong? There was much he didn't know about her language. He could easily speak something to hurt her and not realize it. But all he could do now was give the truth as he knew it. "When I first met you at the place of death, I thought you hunted with the Sioux. To kill the People and take my son and daughter."

He'd guessed her expression would close off with those

words, but instead, a glimmer of pain touched her eyes. Hopefully, the truth in this next part would help ease that. "I did not trust you at first, but soon I saw your heart. Your love for my boy and girl. You did not take them from me, you helped me with them. The more I watched, the more I trusted, and the more you came alive inside me."

If he didn't still have one hand in the softness of her hair and the other woven through her fingers, he would have pressed a fist to his chest to show it was his heart most affected by her. Instead, he softened his voice. "I think of you always—when hunting, when sleeping. I did not think you saw me, though. Did not think you liked what you saw."

Her eyes shimmered, and her expression turned harder to read. But he waited, trying to keep his breath even, though his chest tightened with each heartbeat. Should he say more?

The corners of her mouth tugged upward, and she finally spoke. "How could I not like what I see?" She placed her hand on his jaw, her warmth stealing through him. "You're brave and strong and capable, but it was the way you cared for your children that first drew me. You're not afraid to give whatever they need from you. To seek help when you don't know what to do. Even more, you're not afraid to love them. Seeing you, a great warrior, hold your tiny daughter and look at her as though she is everything to you…"

Her eyes glimmered even more, and her hands slid down his neck to rest on his chest. "How could I not be moved? The more I watch you, the more I'm drawn to know you better. I'm sorry for my boldness in kissing you though."

He lifted their joined hands and pressed a kiss to her fingers. "I'm not sorry."

The sound of footsteps grabbed his attention, and he looked behind, pulling away from Elise with the movement.

Ben Lane stepped around the rocks that had blocked them from view of the others, his face a thundercloud of suspicion.

He sent a glare to Goes Ahead, then turned to his sister. "I thought you were with Lola, but when we carried the meat to her, she said you'd come to help with the skinning. I didn't think that the case since I never saw you." That last bit held the weight of censure.

She motioned toward the goat she'd already cut the meat out of. "I did. But guess what, Ben? Goes Ahead just accepted the Lord as his Savior. Isn't that wonderful?"

Ben turned to him, his suspicion shifting into confusion as he blinked. This surely wasn't what he'd expected to learn when he found the two of them alone together. What would he think if his sister told all? That suspicion from a moment before gave a likely answer. Would this choice Goes Ahead made to follow their God change how Ben felt about him?

Ben studied him. When Goes Ahead nodded, a grin touched the man's mouth as he returned an answering nod. The smile looked only a little forced.

Maybe his concern made sense. Ben likely saw the parts of Goes Ahead that Elise had somehow missed. The fact that he was a warrior, raised in the ways of the People.

And she was so...unlike anyone he'd ever met. Delicate, yet strong. A very different raising, yet she easily knew her way around gutting a mountain goat. She came from a family with many little ones as he had...but they'd all lived.

Ben stepped toward them, his smile easier now. "That *is* wonderful. Welcome to God's family. We're both sons of the one true God now. Brothers in Him."

Elise pushed up to her feet. "I'll take the meat from the goat I worked on to Lola. Shall I take any of this?" She surveyed the mutilated carcass before him.

Goes Ahead shifted his attention to his work, where he should have kept it when he first started this task. "I will finish and cut off both hides. We can load the horses and cook the meat when we camp at dark."

As he took up his knife again, the heaviness in Ben's gaze pressed in on him. At last, the man spoke. "All right then. I guess I'll help load the meat and get us ready to move on."

Goes Ahead wasn't sorry to see them go. He needed a few minutes alone when he didn't have to worry about his thoughts showing on his face. Much had changed. He only wished he knew what all the changes would mean.

∾

*E*lise grabbed up another rotten branch from the ground, this one in slightly better shape than the others she'd gathered. Her arms were full now, so she could head back to camp.

Goes Ahead had halted them a little earlier than usual so they could cook the goat meat and clean the hides enough to be packed for travel. Since Lola sat with both sleeping babes and Goes Ahead had insisted his son help care for their horse, Elise volunteered to gather wood for the fire.

She desperately needed a few minutes alone to clear her mind. A few minutes when she didn't have to face her brother's questioning gaze or try not to let herself fall into the wonderful memories of Goes Ahead's kiss. Not an easy feat when the man rode just in front of her all day, his broad shoulders solid and his son tucked securely behind him. Both had captured her heart far too quickly.

The sound of men's voices through the trees down the slope below gave her pause, and she stopped to listen.

Strangers. That definitely wasn't the direction Ben, Goes Ahead, and White Owl had taken the horses to find grazing.

She strained for a glimpse of the strangers or to make out anything they were saying. She knew so little of the tribes' languages, but perhaps she could pick out something.

But they spoke English.

Her heart surged. Americans? They had to be. She and Ben had met very few white men in their work among the tribes, only a few French trappers in one of the Blackfoot camps.

She had to catch the newcomers before they rode away. Maybe these men had come from the States this summer. They would have news from there.

She dropped her load of logs with a clatter, and the voices paused. At least she'd alerted them to her presence so they wouldn't think she was sneaking up on them. She didn't bother trying to walk quietly as she scampered down the hill.

When she rounded the trees to come within sight of the men, she slowed to a more dignified pace. She'd been in this wild land so long, she barely remembered the manners she'd used as she strolled the streets of Marcyville. Americans would expect that from a fellow countryman though. Especially a lady.

By the time she could finally see one of the men through the branches, he was watching her, his gaze squinted between his dark bushy eyebrows and mustache. The deep leathery tan of what skin could be seen proved he'd spent many days in the sun, though Ben was proof a single summer lived outside in this land could do that to a man. So this fellow may still have come west this year.

The horse behind him turned out to be a packhorse, but as she moved close enough to carry on a conversation without having to yell, two more men on horseback with their own packhorses came into view.

She paused about twenty strides away, and the first fellow removed his hat and plopped it on his knee. "Woowee, ma'am. If you ain't a sight for sore eyes. In fact, I'm still not sure I believe what my lookers are tellin' me. Are you really a white woman out here on this mountainside?"

Neither of the other two took off their hats, but the second man's face spread in a toothy grin. The third eyed her as though he expected her to turn into a fellow before his eyes.

He was the next to speak, though his tone wasn't nearly as friendly. "Heard one of the men in that Flathead village say there was a white woman who married up with a Snake Indian roaming in these mountains. Reckon you'd be her."

The man must be speaking of Lola. Some people called the Shoshone tribe Snake Indians. She'd even heard White Owl use the name for his people.

Did he wear such a dour expression because he thought she was already wed? Or that she'd wed one of the natives?

She gave him a kind smile that would hopefully ease his grumpiness. "You might mean my good friend and traveling companion Lola. She is married to a Shoshone brave named White Owl. My name is Elise Lane. My brother and I have been working as missionaries to the tribes since the spring of '31."

The man in front perked up, his brows rising. "Missionaries, you say? What in the world are ya Bible-thumpin' the Indians for? Weren't enough white folks back in the States would listen to you?"

She stiffened but fought to keep anger from appearing on her face. She'd forgotten how hurtful white people could be with their words. But these Americans deserved to be shown the Lord's love as much as the Indians. "We feel God called us to share His good news with those who inhabit this beautiful land, and we've been blessed to see many come to faith in Him." *Many* might be stretching it a bit, depending on his definition of the word.

The fellow nodded, then his gaze moved up the slope she'd descended. "Where's the rest of your group?"

Ben would want to meet these men, to question them about news from the east. And Lola would probably be eager to talk to them too.

She pointed up and around the side of the mountain toward their camp. "Just below that outcropping of rock, beyond those cedars. We'd be honored to host you at our fire."

All three men nodded, and the first nudged his horse forward. "You lead the way."

As she started back to camp, a niggle of unease slid through her pleasure. Ben and Lola would love to hear what these men had to share. But what would the others think?

CHAPTER 12

"*I*'m headed up to camp."

Goes Ahead lifted another log into his already full arms, then turned at Ben's words. White Owl had already started up the slope toward the place they'd left the women and children.

Ben carried a saddle draped over each shoulder as he trudged after the Shoshone. "I'll come back down and gather more wood after I drop these with the rest of our things."

Goes Ahead nodded. "I come too. I will bring Walking Bird with me to gather more wood." If his daughter didn't need him, that was. She often tended to delay his plans.

"The boy seemed more content riding today." Ben glanced back at Goes Ahead when he spoke. "I was teaching him to count in English. He can go all the way to twenty now."

Goes Ahead nodded. Ben wasn't normally so talkative, but there seemed an easiness between them today. At least, from Ben's side. Was it because Goes Ahead had accepted their God? The man had spent extra time that morning reading the Bible and explaining the words before they set out on the trail. He talked a great deal about Jesus and the hard way He had died so others would live.

Goes Ahead had seen warriors die nobly to protect their families. This Jesus had somehow managed to save *all* people with His death, according to Ben.

As they neared the place where they'd left the women to set up camp, the sound of voices drifted from ahead. Those tones were too deep to belong to his son or Elise or Lola. His entire body tensed. The voices spoke in the white man's tongue.

Just ahead of him, White Owl had also snapped to attention. Goes Ahead lengthened his stride and softened his step to approach quietly. White Owl did the same, and he strained to catch words as they approached.

"...back in St. Louis. I heard a set of proper buckskins sells for three times what you can get for the leather. It's the novelty of the thing. Folks get all moon-eyed about seeing the frontier, but no one has the backbone to come live here a spell. They're too afeared about Indian attacks and buffalo stampedes and the like."

Anger swept through Goes Ahead at the spiteful way the man spoke of his people and the land, but the fellow wasn't finished. His voice was louder now that they'd nearly reached him. "Can't say as I blame them. One month in this land is prob'ly worser than any of those tall tales they think up back east."

White Owl raised a hand to halt Goes Ahead as they reached the shrubby trees that concealed them from the speaker. Best they know the situation before they leapt upon the enemy. Ben halted just behind them, but his breathing seemed loud at Goes Ahead's back.

They had to reach forward to shift the needles enough for a clear view as they peered through the branches.

There was White Owl's wife, sitting on the ground with both babes in her arms. The sight of his daughter made his blood pulse harder through his chest. At least the stranger hadn't taken her. Why had Goes ahead left his children alone? He'd thought them safe with Elise and Lola, but he should have known better. They hadn't been safe with Bright Eyes. And these two women weren't even their mother.

He should have kept them both with him. Elise, too, so he could protect her.

He leaned to find his son and Elise, and to get a better glimpse of the enemy. There. Walking Bird sat just in front of Lola, and Elise knelt before the small flame of their campfire. He still couldn't see the man though.

White Owl motioned toward another spot through the branches, and Goes Ahead leaned to see better.

Two white men.

His body went cold, shifting into the almost numb sensation that came when he was preparing for an attack. These white strangers stood within easy reach of his little ones and the woman who meant much to him.

They had weapons aplenty—knives sheathed at their sides and rifles tied over their shoulders—but none pointed at his children.

He drew his tomahawk from the strap at his side, but a hand on his arm gave him pause.

"No, brother. We must speak words of peace first."

Had White Owl taken leave of his senses? Or maybe he thought the two of them were no match for two hairy-faced white men. The Shoshone were not known for their bravery in battle. If White Owl's heart grew faint at the idea, Goes Ahead could handle these strangers by himself.

He jerked his arm from the man's grip. "I will take them myself." He kept his voice low, though he shouldn't have chanced speaking at all.

"No." White Owl responded just as quietly, but with a harder edge to his voice this time. "We must speak peace words.

Creator Father calls us to live at peace with every man if we can. We cannot attack unless they do so first."

Goes Ahead slid a look at the man. Live at peace with all men? That was impossible, and a God who knew all, like he said, would know this to be true.

"He's right," Ben whispered. "God made and loves them just as He does us. He wishes all His people to live together in peace. We should speak with them first before assuming they're a threat."

Anger rose inside him again, but he did his best to contain it. He'd agreed to follow this God, too, but could he walk blindly into danger? A danger that put his children at risk?

Perhaps he could at least hear what they had to say. But he would not stand by with a hand over his eyes if they drew weapons.

Ben was already stepping around him, pushing through the trees to make their presence known.

Whatever the men had been saying stopped as the three of them stepped into the camp. Elise rose and sent a smile their way, her gaze landing on her brother.

Goes Ahead moved into a position between the men and his children, and White Owl also stationed himself as a barrier in front of his wife and daughter.

Elise's voice sounded bright when she spoke. "Look, we have visitors." She motioned toward the scraggly men. "Malcolm Vesper and Oliver Abrams, this is my brother, Ben Lane, and our good friends Goes Ahead and White Owl."

When she turned back to the three of them, her smile seemed to hold only pleasure, not a hint of worry or any other sign that she thought these men might be a threat. Did she not realize how easily a man could pull out a knife and stab it into one of his children's bodies?

Maybe she hadn't seen as much killing in her life as he had.

That anger tried to surge again, but this time, Elise was included in its target. He did his best to press it down again.

She motioned toward the strangers. "Mr. Vesper and Mr. Abrams came west the spring we did, but they've met with some Americans this year, so they have news from the States. It was good I heard them talking while I was out gathering wood, or we might have missed them completely."

As Ben turned to the men and spoke some kind of welcome, Goes Ahead studied them. They weren't gray-haired, but he wasn't good at deciphering white men's ages when they had so much scruff covering their faces. Maybe a few winters older than himself. They wore the usual clothing of the trappers, with one adding on a blue cloth tunic.

Goes Ahead shifted his focus to decipher what the man in the blue said.

"...decided there weren't enough meat west of the Rockies, 'less a fella considers fish to be meat, which I don't. So we figured on crossin' the mountains afore the worst of winter hits. We'll find us a little sheltered valley near a river or lake, an' hole up 'til spring."

His gaze shifted to Elise just long enough to make Goes Ahead want to move in front of her too, though that would leave his children unprotected. Then the fellow refocused on Ben as he spoke. "A stroke o' luck we found your pretty sister there. She found us, rather. Kendall was prattlin' on about some such and we might never a' heard her if she hadn't called out."

The man's words seemed to both drag and rush on, so Goes Ahead struggled to decipher them. Something the stranger said caught Ben's attention though, for he came alert and glanced around behind the intruders.

"Kendall? Is there someone else with you?"

The fellow in the blue tunic glanced behind him. "Kendall Branson. He's the third in our group. Needed to find a private spot before he come to camp."

The way the man glanced at Elise again—with a glint in his eye and a twitch of his beard—made it hard for Goes Ahead not to react.

Elise hadn't missed it. Red crept over her face, and she ducked her gaze downward.

He didn't know enough of the language to understand what in the man's words had caused that reaction, but something had. And the weasel had done it intentionally. He took too much pleasure in her response.

Would this be enough for Ben and White Owl to believe these men were enemies? Neither took a step forward or reached for weapons. Perhaps there must be more talk before they would be convinced. If only the talk wasn't so hard for Goes Ahead to follow.

The other man, the one whose hair was even paler than him in blue, pointed to Goes Ahead and White Owl. "Which of you is the Indian that married up with the white woman? We heard talk of it all summer long. Snake Indian, we was told." The man jabbed a finger toward White Owl. "You look more Snake than him."

Even White Owl went rigid now, though he still didn't reach for a weapon. The man's words were not spoken in respect, but like a boy kicking a dog in his path.

But it was Ben who answered. "Sir, White Owl and his wife Lola have been traveling with us since the spring and have been much help in sharing our Lord's Gospel with the tribes we've met. He has earned my deepest respect, and I must insist any guest in our camp extends him the same."

The fellow's pale brows rose. He didn't answer right away but turned to Goes Ahead. "How about this Indian, Rev? You saved his soul from hellfire and damnation too? Whatever you do, don't leave them alone with your pretty sister. There's too many white men in need of a good woman to waste her on a redskin."

Numbing fury swept over Goes Ahead. He grabbed his tomahawk and raised it in a single well-practiced motion. That insult had not been buried under layers of extra words, and the man had dragged Elise into his stench.

"No!"

He shouldn't have let the word stop him, but his body seemed tuned to Elise's voice, and his arm froze just before flinging the weapon.

Her tone turned hard as she spoke just loudly enough that her words must have been meant only for him. "No fighting. I'll take care of this."

He must have heard her wrong, but before he could decipher what she'd *actually* said, she raised her voice loud enough for all to hear.

"Mr. Vesper. We extended God's kindness to you, invited you into our camp with the intention of offering food and pleasant company. But we must ask that you refrain from insulting us and our good friends."

The man raised his brows at her, no sign of apology on his face. "And we look forward to both the food and the company, ma'am. I meant no disrespect to anyone here, though I'd sure hate to think you were siding with an Indian over a white man. Perhaps you better take my advice to heart."

It felt like his hands were bound behind his back, trying to keep up with the volley of English words and their meanings. He could easily see this man was a snake-bellied weasel. But had enough ill words been said to justify using weapons? Elise turned red once more, but her expression held nothing akin to embarrassment. Only anger.

Ben spoke up, his voice stronger and sterner than Goes Ahead had heard from him. "That will be enough of such talk. We are all equal in God's eyes, Who made every one of us. No race is superior, neither white nor these native friends. We ask you to remember that, sir. And if you can't treat our friends with kindness and respect, it might be better you go on your way."

The man, Vesper, looked at his comrade, and the two eyed each other. Then he turned back to Ben. "Reckon we're not as welcome here as we thought we'd be. We'll take our leave."

He glanced in the general direction of Elise and dipped his chin. "Ma'am." His gaze shifted to Lola, and then up to White Owl. He didn't say anything else, just turned and stomped away from camp, his companion following.

Another man stepped through the branches just before the two reached him. Goes Ahead tensed. This must be the third in their group. His clothing exactly matched that of the leader in blue.

Their murmured voices drifted back, then all three proceeded onward. The newest fellow glanced behind him with a look that seemed to say he would've preferred to stay and keep on friendly terms. But he didn't. And the sooner these hairy-faced white men left, the better. They were just like most of the white men Goes Ahead had met in the past.

Only Elise and Ben and Lola were different.

The sounds of the strangers' heavy tromping had quieted. But that might be because they hid, waiting to exact revenge for being sent away shamefully.

Goes Ahead would make sure they didn't return. Those white weasels would not have a chance to avenge their pride on his children.

He stepped around the fire, then paused and turned back so his voice wouldn't carry. "I will follow to make sure they don't come back." He swept his gaze from Ben to White Owl, who nodded. The man would want to make sure his own family was safe.

A movement from Elise brought his focus to her as she stepped toward him. "I don't think that's necessary. They looked like they wanted nothing more to do with us. I doubt we'll ever see them again."

That look she referred to was exactly the reason he needed to make sure they kept going far away. Why did Elise continue to trust that those men would keep their word? They'd proved themselves without honor by their speech. He couldn't allow them to get near his children again.

And the fact that she would—that she'd brought them in this camp even before he was there to decide if they should be allowed so near his family... He would have to speak to her of that once he knew for sure the strangers were far away.

He spun the direction the men had gone and started after them, moving quickly and silently. No one under his watch—especially his children—would be hurt by those white strangers, even if it took his dying breath to keep them safe.

CHAPTER 13

A war of emotions waged inside Elise. How dare those men insult Goes Ahead so? The one thing she hated more than any other was blind prejudice. She and Ben had experienced it a little on their journey—both from whites and natives. Why couldn't everyone let a person's character stand for itself without worrying over their race or how they lived?

In her experience, men like those wouldn't be dangerous, just insulting. Which meant it was good they'd left, though they'd not yet shared any real news from the States.

Pretty Shield's fussing broke through her thoughts, and she turned to crouch beside Lola to take the babe. "Come here, my sweet one. That didn't go quite like we hoped, did it? It's all right though. All is well." As she settled the precious girl against her chest, she glanced at Lola to see her thoughts on it all.

Lola was adjusting her bodice as though she planned to feed Anna, but she met Elise's gaze. Her expression was hard to read. Maybe they could find a few moments alone this evening to talk.

For now, White Owl and Ben hovered too close as they worked to finish setting up camp, and Elise needed to start food warming for the evening meal. Full bellies always made a situation better.

With Pretty Shield in one arm, she set to work, unwrapping leather bundles to pull out the goat meat they'd smoked. This would be the last of the camas in their supplies, which meant from here on, they would be eating only meat for every meal.

At least they had food. Goes Ahead had seen to that well.

As if summoned by her thoughts, that brave entered the camp—alone, thank goodness. No sign of a scuffle or white captives.

But when she caught his gaze, a thundercloud shadowed his eyes. Was he still so angry with those men? They'd insulted him. Yet somehow she had to show him that God commanded His followers to love even in the face of persecution. Perhaps White Owl could speak with him. He was a master at standing strong in love and kindness even when others spoke ill of him.

But she couldn't expect White Owl to be the only one to show Goes Ahead God's ways. She straightened and searched for what best to say to ease his worries about the men. "Are they gone?"

Instead of answering, he reached down and took Pretty Shield from her arms. It wasn't an unnatural thing for him to do. They often traded the children back and forth as needed for them to accomplish the work around camp or keep the little ones content on the trail.

Yet the possessive way he held her now and the shift in his expression to something unreadable—and very distant—made a new niggle of unease creep through her.

Thankfully, he didn't make her wait long before he explained himself. "You brought those white strangers into our camp. Around my son and daughter."

The niggle spread to a pressing itch that made her want to spring to her feet. It didn't seem fair she should have to face his ire from a kneeling position while he stood. But she had to keep her wits about her. Had to stay calm and help him understand.

She sat back on her heels and tried to give him a gentle, capable smile. "I would never have let them hurt the children. No matter what. Those men possessed poor manners, but they weren't dangerous. Just because they're white doesn't make them bad. Our Lord made them, too, and His Word commands us to welcome strangers and share what we have with them."

Anger flared in his eyes, but he dropped to her level, sitting on his heels and shifting his daughter so he still held her tightly. "But surely His word doesn't command us to risk our children around men who think them no better than dogs."

An ache tightened inside her. Surely Vesper and Abrams didn't think that way about these innocent children.

But maybe she should have been more careful with these precious lives. She and Ben knew what they were risking in this work. White Owl and Lola too. But Walking Bird and Pretty Shield and Anna relied on her—trusted her—not to put them in situations that could hurt them. How could she be God's hands and feet and voice to others *and* still protect the ones in her care?

She swallowed down the lump in her throat. "I'm sorry, Goes Ahead. I should have waited until you and Ben and White Owl returned from the horses before bringing visitors into the camp. I shouldn't have made that decision on my own about your children's safety."

His chin bobbed once. "That is true." Then his jaw locked in place again.

"Will you forgive me?" *Please.* She couldn't bear having him angry with her. Couldn't bear the thought that she might have endangered these sweet little ones who'd taken over part of her heart. Had the risk really been as great as Goes Ahead seemed to think? Even now, she wasn't certain.

But what mattered was that *he* thought she'd done wrong. That *he* thought she would put his children in peril.

A bit of uncertainty crept over his face. "I do not know this *forgive*."

She searched for words to interpret. "Like what God does with the bad things we've done. When we ask him to forgive us, He wipes our bad things away and doesn't remember them anymore. Makes us clean so we can start fresh with Him."

His mouth pressed in a solemn line. What was he thinking? Whether he could put what she'd done behind him?

At last, he gave another single nod. "I will forgive."

Though his expression gave no hint of his thoughts, those three words planted a seed of hope in her chest. But would things between them be as they were before?

~

*D*id the great God struggle as much to forget about the bad things Goes Ahead had done as he struggled now to forget that Elise had put his children in danger?

He guided his stallion between two boulders as they traveled around the mountain toward the path of the rising sun. Both his children finally slept, Walking Bird slumped against his back and Pretty Shield cradled in her sling at his chest.

All this day, Elise had asked to take one of the children to make his load easier, but he couldn't allow it. Not yet. His mind kept replaying the scene of her sitting with his daughter in her arms and his son nearby while those white strangers wandered freely around the camp. She'd not even been focused much on the men as she worked with the food. Either of them could have snatched one of his children and been far away before she could react.

And Goes Ahead hadn't been there to protect them.

That was what he really couldn't forget. Just like when the

Sioux came back to attack the village, he'd not been there to save his wife. Only the shelter of her dead body had kept their daughter alive.

Or was it God Who had saved Pretty Shield from being discovered by the enemy? The words Ben read from the holy Book that morning had talked about God holding His people in the shadow of His wing to protect them from the evil ones. The Sioux had certainly proved evil.

The fact that his tiny daughter was the only one in the village to survive...that took a great power. A power only a great God could wield.

A stirring behind him meant Walking Bird was waking. When Goes Ahead glanced over his shoulder, the boy arched his back in a stretch. The front of his hair stood up from where he'd laid his forehead against Goes Ahead's back. That sleepy look only reminded him more of how young his son was. Should he push harder for the boy to learn the ways of a warrior? Other men of the People did so with boys about Walking Bird's age. But his son didn't seem big enough to begin the challenges that forced a boy to become brave.

"I need to make water." Walking Bird's words ended in a yawn.

Goes Ahead held in a grunt of frustration. The boy needed to stop far more often than anyone else in the group. Should he deny him? He couldn't bring himself to.

He turned the horse toward a bit of ground more level than the rest where grass poked through the thinning snow. At least the animals could graze a little.

He reined in and told the others what was happening as he gripped Walking Bird's hand to help him slide down. Thankfully, no one else needed to dismount.

Walking Bird wobbled as he moved down the trail to accomplish what he needed to.

Goes Ahead's stallion dropped its head to the fodder and

tore chunks of grass with its strong teeth. He nudged the animal forward a few steps, enough to allow the other horses to graze too. There was more here for them to eat than he'd first thought, now that their noses brushed snow away from the growth. Perhaps they should pause here to let the animals rest and eat what they could.

But that would require the entire group to dismount, and getting everyone back on the trail always seemed a feat, especially with the little ones. Pretty Shield would likely awaken when he climbed down—any change in movement usually made her stir. Best to stay in the saddle while the animals ate only a little.

Walking Bird returned, scooping up clumps of grass as he made his way back along the trail. He carried a handful to the stallion's head and held out his hand as the horse took the food. "There. You can have a full belly." The boy had begun to speak English most of the time now, even when he wasn't prompted. Goes Ahead hadn't spoken the Atsina tongue with him much at all lately. He needed to remember to do that.

When Walking Bird had fed the stallion all the grass he collected, he moved up the slope to pick more, then brought it to Elise's horse. "Now for you."

Elise smiled at the boy. "He says 'thank you.'"

"Thank you." Walking Bird repeated to the horse. Though he'd learned a great deal of the white man's words, he didn't always know exactly how to use them.

Impatience pressed through Goes Ahead as his son gathered more grass to feed the other horses, one by one. Walking Bird needed to stretch his legs though, and the horses could use as much food as they could get.

After feeding the last animal, Walking Bird made his way back up the path toward Goes Ahead. He held something in his hand, then he lifted that hand to his mouth. Lola must have given him food, for her horse had been the last he visited.

Walking Bird stopped at his stallion's head once more and fed the animal the last of whatever the boy held in his palm. As the horse nibbled from his son's hand, Walking Bird sent Goes Ahead a smile. "I found berries. He likes them."

Goes Ahead forced a nod, though what he really wanted to do was pull his son up behind him so they could be on their way.

At last, the boy came to the horse's side and reached up. Goes Ahead grasped his arm and lifted, allowing Walking Bird to slide his leg behind him and settle into place. After he glanced back to make sure the others were ready, he nudged the horse forward. The slope of the land said there might be a valley with water on the other side of this mountain. If they pushed hard enough, they could camp in that place this night.

Their group remained silent as the horses picked their way along the curve of the mountainside. In some places, the rock grew steep like a cliff, and he had to turn the animals upward to find better footing as they worked their way around.

"Why is it raining?" Walking Bird's voice sounded smaller than usual behind him.

Goes Ahead scanned the sky. Only the usual clouds of winter floated above them, nothing dark that meant rain would fall soon. And he'd felt no drops. A new wind had picked up though. Perhaps a gust had blown snow on the boy.

Before he could explain that, Walking Bird spoke again. "I am not..." His tone had taken on that whining sound from the early days on the trail. But different...

Goes Ahead glanced back, but could only see the top of the boy's face. Was that his breathing that sounded so quick and loud, or a trick of the wind?

"Father, I..." The boy's voice changed again, this time breathy and dragging.

Worry clogged Goes Ahead's throat, and he pulled back on the reins to halt his horse so he could better see his son.

But as he was turning, the animal shifted its weight and stumbled sideways, scrambling to catch its balance against the angle of the slope. Goes Ahead spun forward once more and pulled upward on his reins to keep its head up. Wherever a horse's head went, its body would follow.

Just as the stallion regained its footing, a strangled cry sounded behind him. Walking Bird pounded Goes Ahead's back in a hard rhythm.

The worry inside him surged into fear as he spun to see what was wrong with his son. The babe's sling fastened over his chest kept him from turning very far, but he could still see the boy thrashing. His hands waved in wild movements, and his head banged against Goes Ahead's back.

"Stop!" Goes Ahead grabbed the boy's shoulder. Had he gone mad? Spent too long in the saddle and was trying to find release for his energy?

But as Walking Bird's head flopped back, and he caught sight of his son's eyes—only the whites showing—realization of what was happening slipped in.

His son had eaten poison.

CHAPTER 14

Goes Ahead's fear turned to panic, gripping his throat and squeezing. He couldn't let the terror stop him from acting.

With one hand keeping his son from falling, he jumped to the ground, then grabbed the boy with both arms and brought him down. Walking Bird's body shook in violent spasms. His eyes rolled back in his head, and his open mouth foamed around his tongue.

He'd seen this before, but it couldn't be the same... His son hadn't been shot with a poison arrow. What else could cause this response? Bile rose in his own belly as he thought through what he had to do. That other time, the awful things he'd done had saved his life. But this wasn't his own body.

It was his only son.

What if he was too rough and hurt the boy? If these spasms were caused by poison, Walking Bird would die for sure if he did nothing.

But what if something else had brought this on?

The boy stopped shaking, and his face turned paler than any white boy's. As though he were dead.

Goes Ahead could barely breathe. His heart plunged in his chest as he dropped to his knees and lowered his son to the ground. He had to do something. If Walking Bird still lived, he had to make his stomach give up the poison inside.

Pretty Shield squirmed in her sling and began to fuss. Maybe he'd squeezed her too much as he'd carried his son.

"What's happened? What's wrong with him?" Elise dropped to her knees on the boy's other side, her hand brushing Walking Bird's hair away from his face.

She looked up at Goes Ahead, her eyes wild with worry. "He's not feverish. Did he hit his head?"

Goes Ahead couldn't wait any longer. He shook his head as he used his fingers to pry open the boy's mouth. "The berries. I think poison."

"What are you doing? Is the poison bad? Maybe he needs something to drink." Her voice grew distant as she turned and called out to someone else. "Bring water. Quick!"

Goes Ahead couldn't focus on her words, had to keep his attention on making his son cast up everything in his belly. With his large fingers, he pressed as far back as he could touch in Walking Bird's mouth, nearly in his throat.

That other time, he'd done so many things to himself to make the retching begin, he couldn't say exactly what had worked. And he'd been half out of his mind anyway. He'd kept only a tiny stream of awareness, enough to know that he had to get rid of the poison to survive.

Walking Bird's body jerked back away from his fingers, his head flailing to the side. A spasm shook his shoulders. Maybe that had been enough to force the poison up his throat.

But then another convulsion pushed through him, snapping his head against the rock.

No. Not the seizing again.

Goes Ahead slid his hand behind his son's head to cushion the blows as the boy's body wrenched one way then the other in horrifyingly steady beats. Panic swelled through him. How did he stop this? He couldn't do the other things he'd planned to try, not when his son's every muscle and joint had seized so tight nothing could get through. Walking Bird's face had paled whiter than snow. He now held a tinge of purple, almost like the berry he'd eaten.

Goes Ahead had to do something. Had to find a way to help his son breathe.

"Walking Bird! Stop. Can you hear me?"

He barely heard Elise's words, barely saw her hands cradling his son's cheek and shoulder. Speaking to the boy wouldn't stop spasms. That he could remember, though only a dim awareness of the memory.

Determination surged through him. He'd saved himself that day, and he would save his son now.

Touching the inside of Walking Bird's throat had only seemed to make things worse, so he turned his focus to the boy's belly. Just the thought of how he might hurt him made his own insides turn. But he had to take action, and this was all he knew to do. It had to help.

He needed both hands though. Elise was trying to pour little bits of water in the boy's mouth, though the way his head jerked with each spasm, much of the liquid sloshed on his face.

Others crouched around them.

"Put something under his head."

"Here's my coat." Ben dropped a fur on the ground and slid it under Walking Bird's head.

"Let me take the baby." Lola reached for him. Rather, for Pretty Shield, still strapped to his chest. He'd not even heard her cries amidst his panic.

He handed over his daughter, then turned back to the boy's belly. After bracing his hands low in Walking Bird's middle, he kept his palms flat and slid them upward, pressing harder as he went. He had to force those berries up and out.

A hand touched his shoulder. "What are you doing?"

He couldn't look up to see what Elise meant, but he did slip a look at his son's face. The jerking had stopped, but the boy lay so still. His body no longer coiled tight, but impossibly loose. As though he was...

Panic rose in his chest, into his throat so he could barely breathe. Had Walking Bird died already? It was too soon. He should have more time to force out the poison.

"Does he still breathe?" He could barely manage the words. He couldn't take his hands off the belly, couldn't stop trying. If there was any chance...

"What is it? Goes Ahead, what are you asking?" Elise's voice came just strong enough to break through the cloud in his mind. Yet she wasn't answering his question.

Realization slipped in.

He'd spoken in the Atsina tongue. His hands had reached the top of the boy's belly, so he shifted them down to the bottom and pushed again as he slid his fingers upward. His mind searched for the words in her language. "Breath. Does he live?"

Her hand moved from his shoulder down to Walking Bird's chest. "Yes. He's breathing. Heavenly Father, keep him breathing. Heal this sweet boy's body. Show us what to do to help him."

She was no longer speaking to him.

She was praying.

He should be praying too, but he couldn't find the words. Did the great God understand Atsina too, or only the white man's tongue?

Save my son. Bring him back to life. It was all he could manage.

As his hands worked upward over Walking Bird's belly a third time, the boy's body began to tighten again. *Not another round of spasms.*

He wasn't doing enough. His son should have begun to retch by now. Maybe turning him onto his belly would help. What position had Goes Ahead been that awful day? He couldn't remember for sure, it had been nearly ten winters before. Maybe he'd been on his knees, bent forward. Not on his back though, surely. He should have thought of that already.

He reached for his son's side. "We need to turn him."

People moved around them, hands stretching in to help keep the boy's head still and turn his feet. Some kind of commotion sounded behind him, but he couldn't turn to see what it was.

Finally, they had Walking Bird positioned on his belly with his face turned to the side. His eyes were open now, though his gaze roamed in the distance. Not focused. He still looked pale, but no longer purple. And his body had relaxed again without jerking into those awful spasms.

Goes Ahead positioned his hands on the boy's back as he had on his belly. Would the pressure have the same effect on his back?

Walking Bird's eyes jerked to him in question. The boy seemed more aware now. Surely that was good.

Goes Ahead spoke in the Salish tongue he would know best. "You must rid yourself of the berries."

His son gave no sign that he understood. He seemed to be watching, but his eyes still held a hazy look. His breathing had grown louder now, as though he struggled for air. Was lying on his belly making it harder?

One push upward, then maybe he would turn him again. Pressing with as much strength as he dared, he slid his hands upward along the boy's back. He had to get the poison out.

But the more strength he used, the louder Walking Bird's breathing grew. The air seemed to rasp from deep inside. The boy gave a strangled cry and his hands moved over the ground. Whatever he was attempting to do, he didn't have the strength.

"Goes Ahead, no. He can't breathe." Elise's hands gripped his wrists, but it didn't take much to withstand her. He had to do this to save his son.

But not even pushing from the back seemed to be helping. Maybe he should try Walking Bird's throat again. Maybe with the boy on his side.

He gripped those small shoulders and shifted his son so he faced him. Walking Bird trembled, though not with those hard convulsions. His face had turned the hue of the berries again, that awful shade worse than death.

The sight blurred in front of Goes Ahead as his eyes filled, but he wiped the liquid on his shoulders so he could see. He couldn't lose Walking Bird. He'd had too little time with his son.

And the time he'd had felt so squandered. He'd not treasured the days.

He wrapped his fingers around the base of the boy's throat loosely, placing his thumbs in that soft spot in the front. He slid them upward as he had his hands on his son's back. There was a spot just below the chin that could sometimes cause the food inside to spew out. If he could find it with his big clumsy hands.

Walking Bird's eyelids had nearly closed now, and his lips were almost black.

Great God save. Please. If You are as real as these others say You are. Save my son.

Once more, tears streaming down his face blurred his view of his son. He didn't wipe them away. He couldn't watch Walking Bird die.

His thumbs had reached the boy's jaw, and he pressed in the hollow part, working his fingers around the area. Feeling for any place that would cause the action he needed.

Even through his tears, he saw the lad's eyes pop wide. His mouth gaped, his lower jaw swinging open then almost closing, then gaping again. His throat grew tight beneath Goes Ahead's fingers. *No more spasms. Please.*

Walking Bird turned his face toward the ground, and the trembling in his shoulders grew stronger. A new round of terror roared through Goes Ahead. No. This couldn't be the end.

Walking Bird jerked, then something spewed out of his mouth. A rush of foul-looking liquid, as dark as the boy's lips had been a moment before, spewed onto the coat beneath him.

A reaction swarmed through Goes Ahead, stronger than anything he had felt before. Relief and gratitude and so much more.

Elise rubbed Walking Bird's back, her voice a steady soothing stream. Goes Ahead couldn't do anything but watch as the river that flowed from his son's mouth slowed to a trickle. Had enough come out? Was there more of the berry left inside him?

"Can we build a fire here?" Elise's voice pulled him from his thoughts. "I think he needs water and to get warm. His body has been through a great deal."

"This one cannot go farther now either."

Goes Ahead glanced over his shoulder to find the other voice. White Owl crouched by a horse on the ground. A heartbeat passed before he recognized the animal—his own stallion. The horse lay on the rocky slope with its head up, nose resting on the ground as if it were sleeping.

He opened his mouth to ask what happened, but realization sank in. The berries.

He glanced around the rest of the group. "Did anyone else eat them?"

Elise shook her head. "Only Walking Bird and the horse. Can we build a fire here?"

She'd taken off her coat and laid it over his son. He should have been the one to do that. The air had dropped cold enough that their breath clouded in front of them. When had that happened?

"I'll find firewood." Ben stood, then turned and scanned the area.

Goes Ahead had to regain his senses. They had much to do here. Elise had curled around his son, and the boy responded to whatever she said, though her words were not loud enough for him to make out.

He could leave them for a minute while he built a fire and gathered water. There didn't look to be a level spot, but they would have to rest here a while. Once he'd made his son comfortable, he also needed to see to his horse. At least White Owl was with the animal for now.

He'd never been so grateful for all these people traveling with him. For Lola, yes. He'd been thankful for her the very first time she fed his daughter. And Elise, though her actions with those white strangers had made him wary. But she comforted his son so well.

It didn't take long to lay a fire with the kindling they carried. Ben had gone down the mountain in search of wood and now carried an armload back toward them. They would need even more than that if they stayed in this place through the night.

Walking Bird had to rest, but could they find a better camp before dark came? The weight of responsibility pressing on his shoulders had never felt so strong. Walking Bird lived through the poisoning—so far, at least.

Yet why did it feel like with every success there was so much more at stake?

CHAPTER 15

*E*lise had been fighting back tears all afternoon. Tears for Walking Bird, for what had almost happened to this sweet boy. As she cradled him in her lap now, his head against her shoulder and several layers of furs covering him, that sharp burn sprang to her eyes once more.

The helplessness when Walking Bird's body had been caught up in the seizures...that had been awful. One of the worst moments she could remember.

And the sight of Goes Ahead with his hands clamped around his son's throat. She squeezed her eyes against the memory. Had he thought choking the lad would save his life? Maybe it had, but still...the thought that he could do such. Those powerful arms could have squeezed just a bit too hard, and he might have killed his son or destroyed something vital in his throat. How could he have taken that chance?

On this journey she'd seen so much of his heart she'd felt like she really knew the man. But did she in truth? How could she trust him implicitly in such a short time?

She couldn't. She *shouldn't*.

He surely hadn't meant to hurt his son. He'd been desperate and had done what he thought best to help him.

And it had worked. That should be enough.

But she couldn't ignore the reality of how very dangerous life in this wild country could be. Goes Ahead was used to these challenges, both from nature and from battles with other tribes. How many people had those strong hands killed in the past? Even with his new faith, the habits and actions that were ingrained in him couldn't be wiped away overnight. Not unless God chose to provide a miracle, but in her experience, the Lord usually preferred to help a person grow in their faith over time as they learned how to accept His love and let it pour out to others.

Still, that didn't change the hardships here. If she married him, how many of their children would be lost like Goes Ahead's siblings? Or if they returned to Marcyville, how could his warrior ways not cause problems? She understood his heart, but if that scene had taken place on Main Street in front of a crowd of mothers with their civilized sensibilities, he might have been strung up and hanged. Or at least ostracized.

How could they ever make this work?

Maybe it was best she guard her heart. Even more now since they'd shared that kiss. No wonder such intimacies were usually saved for the end of a courtship when a couple knew marriage was their next step.

At the moment, Goes Ahead knelt beside his sick horse, and only the murmur of his and White Owl's voices drifted to her. It sounded like they were speaking in one of their common languages. Probably Salish. White Owl had become quite versed in that tongue through the summer, and of course Goes Ahead had married into that tribe. Walking Bird had picked up English quickly, but he slipped back into his Salish when he was sleepy or afraid. If he spoke now, that would probably be the language he would use.

But the boy didn't speak, only sat impossibly still in her lap as she cradled and rocked him. His body felt too rigid for him to be asleep. Surely he was exhausted from the ordeal. But fear must be wrapped around him too.

Goes Ahead stood, leaving White Owl by the horse's side with a final word. Then he strode toward her, and she tried to catch his gaze, but his focus was on the bundle in her lap. He'd been busy building a fire, laying evergreen needles over the mess that had spewed from the boy's mouth so none of the animals would eat there, and tending the horse. He hadn't had time to sit quietly with his son to see for sure that he was doing better.

As he crouched in front of them, she asked, "How is your horse?" He seemed concerned, but not distraught, which made her think the animal wasn't dying. But would a brave show such emotion? She wasn't sure.

He'd certainly been upset about his son—she would never forget the way the tears flowed down his face as he tried to get the boy to cast up the poison. But the stallion might only be a tool to him. The method he used to travel from one place to another, like his bow and arrows were his means to hunt.

And the horse might also be a symbol of wealth. He'd said as much when he spoke of the trade Bright Eyes's father offered for her hand. Elise had to be careful in ascribing gentle motives to his actions.

He still didn't meet her gaze as he answered. "He is unwell, but I think rest is what he needs." He reached for his son, and she forced herself to hand him over. It felt so good to have the boy snuggled close and warm. But his father needed this time with him.

Goes Ahead rose to standing with the lad perched on his arm, letting the furs fall away. The boy wore the cloak she'd given him, though, so he should be warm enough, especially held close to his father.

He talked to Walking Bird using the language she couldn't understand. That shouldn't make her feel left out. After all, they only spoke English around her as a courtesy. Yet this was one more proof that she and Goes Ahead came from very different worlds.

Walking Bird answered his father in a quiet voice, but at least he was speaking.

She should leave them alone and set to work. She had much to do. And perhaps she could pull Ben aside for a few minutes to talk. Her brother might be overly-protective, but he also possessed a healthy dose of good sense. She needed better counsel than her own muddled thoughts. *Lord, give me wisdom.*

Yet as she pushed to her feet and looked toward the tasks that needed her attention, she couldn't shake the feeling that turning away from Goes Ahead and his family would mean losing her best chance at happiness.

But she wasn't certain how to grasp that happiness.

Or if she even should.

~

"That sure was a miracle how Walking Bird threw up the berries just in time. I wasn't sure how much longer his little body would last."

Goes Ahead nodded in response to Ben's statement as they sat around the fire, eating the warm stew Elise had prepared for the evening meal. Walking Bird slept on his bed, tucked in his furs. Hopefully this rest was what he needed to recover fully.

Ben was looking at Goes Ahead, waiting for him to answer. He'd not heard the word *miracle* before but could guess it meant something wonderful, based on the rest of the man's words.

Yet his weary mind struggled to find the right thing to say in their tongue. At last, a few thoughts came. "It was the only thing

I could think to do. Last time, that was what worked. Though I didn't remember it until after."

Ben's chin lifted. "Last time?"

He hadn't meant to bring up that old day. But perhaps it would not be wrong to speak of it. "When I still lived in my father's village. I went with my friend to hunt. He was not careful with his arrow, and it struck my belly." He pressed a hand to the place. "Any man shot with an arrow dipped in the poison of a rattlesnake will die. Catch the Wind was very sad. He could not watch me die from his mistake, so he left to tell my family."

Goes Ahead couldn't help sliding a glance at Elise. Would she remember that he was the only surviving son? Would she suspect that his mother had sunk into grief at hearing that her last child no longer lived? His father and mother had believed Catch the Wind's words so fully, they hadn't even come to see the truth for themselves. Catch the Wind had returned later that night to bring back Goes Ahead's body but had been amazed to find he lived.

"What happened?" Ben leaned forward, elbows propped on his knees. "You're still alive, so it sounds like maybe you experienced a miracle too."

A miracle? No, it hadn't been wonderful. That day had been so awful, he still saw it sometimes in his dreams and awoke covered with sweat. "I knew I had to spew the poison out of my body. I hoped if I could bring up everything in my belly, I would be spared. I do not remember everything I tried, but I think what finally brought the poison out of my mouth was the last thing I did today for my son."

"That sounds awful." Lola sat with a plate in her lap while White Owl held their daughter beside her. "Had you already taken ill from the poison, or did you stop it early enough?"

He shook his head, as much to shake away the attack of

memories as anything. "The poison begins to kill very soon. I shook and jerked like my son did this day."

Once more, he allowed a glance at Elise to see how she responded to the story. She hadn't said anything, and she'd positioned herself on the other side of her brother during the meal. What did that mean?

A gully seemed to have spread between them. A distance he couldn't see but could feel. Was this what she wanted? To pull away from him? Perhaps she realized how different they were. White Owl and Lola made it work, but Goes Ahead was a warrior of the White Clay People. He killed far more than any Shoshone warrior could have. He was a different man from White Owl, and Elise was...too delicate...too good to be tied to the likes of him.

Yet something inside tightened at the thought of losing her. The two of them together did not make sense, but that didn't stop him from wanting it. He would need to control that desire.

When they'd finished the meal, quiet settled over the group. Both his children lay sleeping on their mats. He needed time alone, time to gather his thoughts and ease the tightness inside him. Pretty Shield might wake again to eat before she settled for the night, but Walking Bird seemed to be sleeping so deeply, he wouldn't need to worry about the boy rousing while he was gone.

He looked to Lola. "I am going to scout around our camp. I can take my daughter." He could not assume she would care for the babe, but if she offered to, he would accept.

"Let her sleep. If she awakens, she'll be hungry. I'll be here to care for her. Walking Bird too. Sleep is what they both need."

He nodded and rose, and as he turned into the darkness, he made sure his tomahawk and knife were secure in their straps. Likely he would meet no dangers, but he would be prepared in case he did.

He moved up the slope instead of following the path they'd

been taking around the mountain. He could have gone downward and gathered more wood for the fire. Maybe he would do that before he returned to camp, but first, he needed the effort climbing required. And the farther up he traveled, the closer he felt to the land. To the mountain itself. And maybe to the God Who created it?

There was so much he didn't know of this God. But as he watched Ben and the others, it seemed he lacked more than just understanding. Not only did they know *about* this God, they seemed to know *Him*. To be able to speak with Him and hear from Him.

He wanted that. And maybe he had to be the one to begin their conversation.

He didn't have enough time to climb all the way to the peak —he had to get back to his children—but he reached a place where the rock jutted out. When he stepped up onto that high spot, the wind whipped around him, swiping hair across his face, then away again. The wind possessed the freedom to fly anywhere it pleased, as fast as it chose. The wind could tear down or the wind could mold, smoothing rock and winding rivers.

But maybe the wind's freedom wasn't as great as it seemed. Did the God who created the air and forced it to blow also guide these gusts with the full strength of His hand? And had that same God forced Walking Bird to cast up the poison at the very last moment before it took the boy's life?

God had that power. The more Goes Ahead heard the Scriptures Ben read each morning, the more certain he was that the God who created this world still possessed that same power.

So why hadn't He made the berries spew from Walking Bird right away, before the boy suffered so much? Why had He waited until the last breath before death? Or why had He allowed Walking Bird to find the berries at all?

Perhaps Goes Ahead should simply be grateful his son had

lived. And he was—more thankful than he could say. But the questions still lingered.

Perhaps it was time to ask the Creator Himself. He raised his focus to the distant sky. Clouds covered most of the stars, but a few peeked through. "If You hear me, I am Goes Ahead, son of He Who Speaks Loud of the White Clay People." Perhaps he didn't need to say that. The God who made him would know his name.

He lifted his chin. "You know me. But we are not equal in this. I do not know You as I wish to. I have not heard You speak. But speak now, if You will. Tell me why You allowed my son to eat the poison berries. If You are strong enough to guide the wind, why could You not guide his eyes away from them?"

He waited as the gusts tugged at him, slipping icy tendrils beneath his coat. Would the voice come in the cry of the wind?

My son.

The thought crept in before Goes Away made sense of it. Those were his own words, what he'd said about Walking Bird, but they took on a different sound in his mind. As though spoken by another.

He focused on the darkness above. "My son, the one I committed to keep safe. Is it that I should have done better to protect him?"

My son.

Again those words in his mind, but this time stronger. Almost like an echo of someone else's voice.

I am Creator.

This time the thought slipped in just like one of his own. Yet it wasn't his thought. Goes Ahead, son of He Who Speaks Loud of the White Clay People, had not formed bone and flesh to make the child. Though he was his father, he'd not reached into his wife's womb and molded the babe.

God had done that. Did that mean this voice was God's?

My son, the one I created.

Understanding swept through him with a strength that nearly pressed him back a step. God had created Walking Bird, this he already knew. But what did that really mean? God knew more about his son than Goes Ahead did. Far more probably, for it seemed he had so much to learn. And when man made something with his own hands, he would be proud of his creation. He would want the best for it.

That must be the same with God.

So how could the best mean allowing Walking Bird to endure such pain?

When he raised his eyes to the heavens again, God didn't feel as distant. "If You want good for this boy, why didn't You protect him?"

As he waited, he did his best to listen for another clear thought in his mind. An impression that felt different from his own ideas.

Nothing came. Was there another way God might speak? Or did He not have an answer to this hard question? White Owl said God sometimes used the Scriptures Ben read to them, His words, to show His people the good path. Was there something Ben had read that could answer this question?

He'd not focused on remembering specific words, only the ideas in the book. Those were hard enough to understand, to reshape the way he thought of God and his understanding of the way God thought of him.

But there had been that story of Jesus. Yes, He had been speaking to those who walked with Him. He had said that there would be troubles in this life. Hard things. But we should not be sad because Creator Father was stronger than any hard thing.

That thought didn't ease the knot inside Goes Ahead as much as he'd hoped. Hard things happened so God could show His strength? That didn't seem to fit with the loving God Who cared about those He made. So which was true?

He waited a little longer in the whipping wind, staring out over the slopes around him, their peaks rising into the clouds.

He needed to get back to camp. And his spirit did feel a bit easier than before.

He lifted his gaze to the sky once more. "We will speak more later." Perhaps he should be satisfied with those few words pressed into his spirit.

But he wanted to know all. Wanted to understand this God he'd committed to follow.

CHAPTER 16

*A*fter his brief conversation with God on the mountain, Goes Ahead moved lower on the mountain and loaded his arms with firewood. He turned up the slope toward the camp, but he'd only taken a few steps when voices sounded along the path ahead of him.

"I don't know, Benji. He's certainly a different man from who I thought he was when we first met him."

Goes Ahead froze. That was Elise's voice, and she sometimes called her brother by that name. They were speaking of someone else—Goes Ahead or White Owl?

She continued talking, so he strained to hear more. "And now that he's come to believe, he'll change even more as he grows in his faith."

She became quiet, but Ben didn't answer. Her tone had sounded like she was asking a question, though her words hadn't voiced one.

Finally, Ben spoke. "I think you need to be careful. You two are from different worlds. Sure, he's a Christian now and I'm thankful. But that doesn't mean I'd hand you over to him. Really, Lisi. Think what you're saying."

They were speaking of him. How much had Elise told her brother of what had happened between them? In truth, it wasn't so much. A kiss, nothing more.

But it had meant more to him. And she seemed to feel the same. He'd thought so, at least.

The fact that she was now speaking of him to her brother must mean she did. Though she didn't sound certain.

But by Ben's response, he didn't think they would make a good match. Anger tried to rise up inside Goes Ahead, but he pushed it aside. Hadn't he questioned that very thing? This was no trade of horses for a marriage.

No, this would be a hard match. Elise might be accepted in time among his people, but learning their ways might challenge her. And could he really expect her to leave her life for his? It should be the other way. Could he stomach the thought of living in the white man's land?

Even the idea formed a knot in his belly. Maybe Ben was right. Their worlds were far too different.

Brother and sister had been silent as his thoughts took over, but Elise spoke again. "I'll think about it."

She didn't say no. Hope rose in his chest. Maybe her brother's words hadn't turned her against him. Maybe she'd felt the strength of what had begun to grow between them.

Should he let her go if she chose to? Or fight for what they could become?

He'd never been one to back down, even when he faced a large war party alone. Warriors of the White Clay People fought for what they wanted. They reclaimed anything stolen from them.

No, he wouldn't let Elise go so easily. He would win her heart if she would give it.

⌢

"*C*ome, my son. We must move to a better camp." Goes Ahead reached for Walking Bird's hand to help him to his feet. Part of him wanted to lift the boy into his arms and carry him. His son still looked so pale. Though he'd walked around a little when the sun first rose, he'd only eaten a bite of the meat Elise cooked. He would need more than that to regain his energy, but hopefully later this day he could manage another small meal.

As they turned to start down the slope behind the others, Walking Bird wobbled on his feet. Goes Ahead placed a hand on the boy's shoulder to steady him. They'd spent the night in this place where his son took sick, but they would need to wait another sleep for the boy and horse to recover enough to travel far. They moved to a better camp, farther down the mountain where the wind wouldn't snuff out their fire and closer to grazing and water for the horses. So far, they'd found plenty of clean snow to melt for their cooking water.

Walking Bird didn't speak as they followed the steps of the others, though his path wavered, his feet sometimes stumbling, even with Goes Ahead's hand steadying him. Yet the boy didn't complain as he'd done those first days on the trail. Had it taken something so awful as nearly dying to make him thankful for each step, no matter how hard?

Maybe. Though a boy who'd lived only four winters might not think such deep thoughts.

At last, they reached the place of the new camp. Ben carried logs that still glowed red with fire on their ends, and he now crouched to nurture the flames back to life.

"I'll make beds for the little ones." Lola kicked snow aside to clear a space, then reached for the stack of furs White Owl carried. Their daughter nestled in the cradleboard on her father's back, her wide eyes taking in the rest of them as White Owl moved around, unloading the supplies he'd carried.

Goes Ahead stood with his son as Lola and Elise laid out the furs. Elise wore Pretty Shield strapped in her sling, but the way his daughter's hands waved, she wasn't sleeping. He needed to build a real cradleboard for her instead of the sling she was quickly growing out of. How did she seem so much bigger now than when they'd left the Salish camp?

A cradleboard would have to wait until they reached his father's village. He didn't have the time or tools to fasten a proper one now.

He should be helping the women prepare the beds instead of standing there watching, but Walking Bird still wavered on his feet. He might fall if Goes Ahead pulled his hands away. Before this journey, he would never have felt guilty for standing by and watching what he'd always considered women's work.

But everything in his life had been turned on end. The care for his children was his responsibility, and that meant making their beds. He had no wife to handle such matters.

He stepped forward, guiding Walking Bird beside him. He crouched next to the remaining rolled furs and kept one arm around his son while he used his free hand to lay out the pallet.

Elise moved to the opposite side and helped spread the pelts, though she didn't look at him.

He had to talk with her. This day. He had to find a way to speak his thoughts without the others overhearing. Maybe if Walking Bird slept again, he could ask her to check the stallion with him.

At last, he helped his son stretch out on the furs, then covered the boy. Walking Bird clutched his belly and looked up at Goes Ahead with weak eyes. He spoke in Salish. "I hurt."

Goes Ahead's own body ached with the pain the boy had endured. "I know, my son. Rest. Can you eat now?"

The boy shook his head, and his eyelids lowered. He didn't speak again, and sleep seemed to take him quickly, even as Goes Ahead stayed beside him.

When he stood and turned away from the boy to find Elise, she was standing a little distance back, watching his son. Her eyes glimmered, and her mouth pinched in sadness.

Again, pain pressed in his chest. How could he be a great warrior and still allow so much sadness to come to those he loved?

And he must love Elise, for as he watched her now, the ache for her to be happy was as strong as that for his children. He needed to find out what had come between them. Then he could find a way to reach her again.

She turned away before he could speak to her, pulling out the food bundles.

He moved to her side and knelt beside her. "I can take the babe with me to find more firewood."

She still didn't look at him as she shook her head. "She's content. Your load will be lighter without her. If she grows restless, I'll lay her on her fur with a toy."

"Surely your work will be easier without her. I can lay her down now." Anything he could do to help Elise.

She shrugged. "If you like."

She slipped the strap over her head and handed over the bundle of his daughter and her sling. As he took the babe, his hands brushed Elise's. Warmth surged up his arms, and his gaze jerked to hers.

She still wouldn't look at him, and the knot of worry in his throat grew tighter. He had to do something. "Elise."

"Yes?" She occupied herself with pulling the trade blanket snug around Pretty Shield, though she was careful not to touch him.

"When I return with the wood, will you walk with me to check my horse? I wish to know what you think." And not only about the stallion. But if he told her his real reason, she might refuse to go, if the way she avoided him now was any measure.

"I..." Her gaze darted up to bounce off his before returning to his daughter. "If you need me to."

He nodded. Desperately, he needed her to hear him.

Pretty Shield stared up at him with those dark, trusting eyes as he carried her to the bed pallet. When he laid her down, her arms struggled to pull out from the blanket around her.

He helped her free her hands, then tucked the cover tighter around the rest of her. "You might like to be free, but not at the cost of staying warm and safe."

She regarded him with such a solemn expression, almost as if his words made her worry. He didn't *want* his children to worry. They should be happy and strong and curious. How could he help her smile?

Elise had made the babe smile once simply by swiping a rabbit skin against her cheek in a game. He had no rabbit skin, but the fur she lay on was a soft wolf pelt. Maybe he could do the same.

Taking up a loose corner, he stroked it down her cheek, wiggling a little to make the hair tickle her skin. Her eyes lit as though she wanted to smile but needed a bit more coaxing.

"Does that feel soft?" He wiggled it across her neck.

Her gaze moved over his face, and her arms flapped. Still no smile, but she seemed to be saying she wanted more.

"Does this make you happy?" This time he swiped the fur down her other cheek. She kept her focus on him.

Could he do or say something that would pull a smile? He widened his eyes, formed an O with his mouth like Bright Eyes used to do when she played with babies. One of his daughter's cheeks appled, drawing that side of her mouth upward. Could that be called a smile? It didn't feel like a full grin. Not the kind that showed true pleasure.

He squeezed his eyes shut, then opened them wide again, dropping his jaw to make his face seem long. The other side of her mouth tugged this time. He was getting closer, but not quite there.

He grinned and tapped a light finger to her nose. "You're a challenge, daughter. I'll have to learn what pleases you most."

Both corners of her mouth flicked upward, and a glimmer of happiness lit her eyes. Just a quick expression, but definitely pleasure. Maybe it was the touch or maybe his own smile, but she'd shown happiness. Now *he* couldn't stop grinning.

"All right, my songbird. I will return soon." He tapped her nose once more, then stood. First a quick load of firewood, then he had another challenge to meet. And he had a feeling the woman might be far harder to win over than his sweet daughter.

CHAPTER 17

*E*lise's chest ached as the images of Goes Ahead playing with his daughter paraded again and again through her mind. The love that made such a strong warrior drop to his knees and contort his face into strange expressions just to make his infant daughter smile... What would it be like to feel such devotion?

She squeezed her eyes shut, fighting the burn that assaulted them. That day in his arms—during the kiss and after—she'd felt the strength of his regard. How intensely he worked to accomplish what he set out to do. He'd made her feel like the only woman who mattered. No longer Elise Marie Lane, fifth daughter in a line of twelve children.

But Elise, chosen by this warrior who could surely have any woman he fancied.

And chosen by God.

She couldn't forget that her real identity was the daughter of the King of Heaven. She didn't need a man to make her feel special. Her heavenly Father did that, and she'd committed to serve Him by sharing that acceptance and love with people who might otherwise not ever have the chance to learn of Him.

With that reminder shoring up her heart, she was ready when Goes Ahead returned with an armload of wood. A few of the pieces showed fresh ax marks at the ends where he'd cut them down to fit inside the ring of stones surrounding their fire. A small kindness perhaps, but not something she could have managed herself. She could never manage to cut anything substantial with the half-sized ax Ben carried.

As Goes Ahead bent to pick up his daughter, Elise stood and brushed the grass from her skirt. He tucked the babe into her sling and slid the strap over his head. "Your brother and Lola and White Owl are by the stream. They are coming now to stay with Walking Bird."

She nodded as her eyes slid to the boy. Though his sleep seemed peaceful, his features were still so pale, almost lifeless. A weight pressed in her chest.

Goes Ahead waited for her, so she stepped forward toward the path that led to where they'd staked the horses. She didn't meet his gaze, though the pressure of his attention followed her. She couldn't look him in the eyes without her expression giving away her thoughts. Or maybe not her thoughts as much as her heart.

Ben was right. She'd finally accepted that truth. She and Goes Ahead were from two different worlds. They could never form a happy life together. She couldn't imagine herself settled forever in an Indian village, wearing buckskin dresses and cooking over campfires for the rest of her days. And she couldn't form any image in her mind of how Goes Ahead might live if he came east with her.

Another picture slipped in, though. The memory of this man who now walked beside her, kneeling over his tiny daughter. That sweet smile on Pretty Shield's precious face, the grin he'd worked so hard to summon. And the way he'd kept a protective hand around his son's shoulders as they moved to this camp, then helped the boy lay down with such gentleness.

Instead of imagining herself in a camp surrounded by Gros Ventre people she didn't know, if she replaced those pictures with images of this man and his children...

But then her mind flashed with the memory of Goes Ahead and his hands around his son's throat.

Maybe this was all fanciful daydreams. She had only met him a few short weeks ago. She still didn't really know him.

As they reached the patch of meadow where the horses tore into the grass with fervor, it took a second to find Goes Ahead's stallion. The sturdy mount stood a little separate from the others, not grazing but with his head drooped.

She moved toward him, extending her hand for him to sniff her if he wanted to. The stallions she'd met in the past tended to be more high-strung and harder to handle than other horses, but this boy rarely showed those tendencies. Maybe because he was ridden daily, or perhaps Goes Ahead was simply a better trainer.

Still, she would always be cautious around him.

But the horse didn't lift his head at her approach, only flicked an ear toward her as she touched him.

"Hi there, fellow." She rubbed a hand down his shoulder. The stallion lifted his head a bit and turned to eye her, so she stroked his neck, sliding her fingers up to that spot where most horses loved to be scratched behind the ears.

His eyelids drifted half-shut as she rubbed, then finally he let out a heavy breath and dropped his head to nip at a few pieces of grass.

"You were the medicine he needed." Goes Ahead's voice sounded deep and much closer behind her than she'd expected.

Her instinct turned her before she could stop herself. He stood only an arm's length away, and his gaze was impossible to look away from. Her chest squeezed too tight for air to pass through.

Oh, she loved this man. Loved the goodness he showed

every day. Loved the way he was looking at her now like she mattered to him.

But love wouldn't change the fact of their differences. A connection could never work between them. She did her best to strengthen her resistance again.

"Elise. What happened between us before has been always in my thoughts, though much has happened since then." He seemed to gather himself, though he didn't actually move. "At times, I think the places we come from are too far apart. I do not know how I could live among the white men. I don't know if there would be hunting and if I could protect my children from those who would hurt us. I do not know the land. And that not knowing makes me want to keep my son and daughter in the place I am sure of."

His gaze sank into hers a little more as he released a pent-up breath. "But when I think of losing you, of watching you ride away when we reach the village of my father, I know what is between us is not a small thing. Will you give me a chance to prove I can be the warrior of your heart?"

She wanted to say yes. Every part of her longed to bring a smile to those dark eyes.

But she had to hold fast. For once, she couldn't let her heart make her choices. And somehow, she had to say no in a way that didn't hurt him.

Lord, give me the right words. She inhaled a breath and let it out. No magic speech crept onto her tongue. She could only speak the truth. *Don't let me hurt him, Father.*

She couldn't quite meet his gaze, so she focused on the stain on the buckskin covering his right shoulder. "Goes Ahead, I too have been thinking a great deal since that…uh…since the other day. You're a remarkable man, and you and the children have become very special to me." *Lord, give me strength.* It took everything in her to keep the tears clogging her throat from making her voice quiver. And she couldn't let them rise to her eyes where they'd be visible. "I think we're too different. We're from two separate countries. Different cultures and different ways of living. I think it's best we not grow any closer than we already have."

She swallowed to force down the emotions enough to breathe. She'd been the one to start that kiss, which meant she had to say more. "I'm sorry I began something that isn't wise for us to continue. I should have thought through my actions before following my—" She bit back the last words. No sense in speaking aloud that he possessed so much of her heart. That would only make this harder.

He was quiet for too many thundering beats of her heart. Did he expect her to say more? She couldn't bear being with him much longer, not when her insides were shattering.

At last, he spoke. "Elise…"

He sounded like he was going to say something else, but her name in his deep tone was too much to bear.

She shook her head. "I'm sorry. I need to get back to camp." She plunged forward, moving far enough around him that he couldn't reach out and stop her if he wanted to.

But he didn't try.

She'd succeeded in her goal—to break things off. But she wasn't sure her heart would survive the separation.

∾

Goes Ahead had to get away.

Being in this camp, around all these people— around Elise—was too hard.

He'd not been enough for her. She felt this bond they shared, he'd seen it in her eyes from the moment she'd looked at him when they spoke earlier. But he'd not been able to convince her to see if they could make this work between them.

His spirit craved a chance to escape this place, to run like the wind until he became one with the land, or maybe even to slam his ax into a tree over and over until he'd spent the energy coursing through him. But he'd been tied to this little campfire all day because of his children.

Walking Bird slept a great deal through the afternoon, though he now sat up on his fur, eating meat Lola had prepared for him. The boy looked more like his usual self.

Thank you, Creator Father, for bringing him back fully.

Pretty Shield now gave the greater challenge. The babe had fussed and complained all through the going down of the sun. He had no good reason, aside from a desire to flee, to leave his children's care to others, so he'd been tied to this tiny plot of ground.

His daughter had finally quieted to nurse, which gave him enough time to tie some furs above the fire and the bed pallets. The sky showed that rain would fall soon, and the flashes of lightning had already begun in the distance.

Ben helped him secure the coverings quickly, which meant they were done before White Owl returned from walking with his tiny sleeping daughter. Elise had gone from camp too. He'd not heard her say where she went, but he had a feeling she only wanted time away from him.

Better for both of them. At least he didn't have to guard his gaze with her away from camp.

As Goes Ahead settled on the fur beside his son, Lola raised Pretty Shield to her shoulder to pat her back as she normally did after feeding. "There. Now are you happy? If you sleep, I think you'll feel much better."

His daughter let out the noise expected after nursing, then squirmed in Lola's arms.

The woman turned to Goes Ahead. "She's had all she wants to eat, but she's fighting sleep. Perhaps if you take her for a walk, she'll succumb like Anna did."

Goes Ahead glanced at Walking Bird. He would be eager to escape this place under the disguise of putting his daughter to sleep, but he couldn't leave his son.

Lola must have guessed his thoughts. "We'll stay here with Walking Bird. White Owl and Ben and I won't leave camp. From the looks of it, this boy is feeling much better and might even want more to eat." She smiled at his son with those last words.

Walking Bird sent her back a shy grin.

Maybe this would be Goes Ahead's chance to walk out some of his frustration. He placed a hand on his son's shoulder to draw the boy's attention. When Walking Bird looked up at him, Goes Ahead spoke in Salish to make sure he understood the importance. "I am going to take care of your sister. You are to stay with these friends. Stay and protect them like a warrior until I return."

Walking Bird gave two hard jerks of his chin. "I will be a warrior."

After giving his own nod, Goes Ahead rose and took his daughter into his arms. He wrapped the trade blanket tighter around her, then added a fur to keep out wind and the cold air of the coming night, as well as the storm the darkness would bring.

He sent another glance to Walking Bird. Perhaps he should take his son with him. Hadn't he vowed to protect these two himself? But stumbling over the mountainside with this icy wind blowing around him couldn't be good for Walking Bird. Already, Pretty Shield had begun to squirm and fuss. Maybe she would give in to sleep soon and they could return quickly. Even the short time away would be good for him and his daughter both, but it could only hurt his son.

Lola caught his gaze. "I'll watch over him carefully."

Goes Ahead nodded. "I will be back soon." As he shifted his daughter into the position she liked best to sleep, he turned and started out, taking a path that wrapped around the mountain instead of climbing upward.

The flash of light in the sky looked nearer this time, and a clap of thunder sounded soon after. Without the glow of the campfire, the thick clouds overhead darkened the evening light to night.

Pretty Shield fought harder in his hold, trying to uncover her arms and resisting his effort to keep her in the sleeping position. Should he let her break free? She needed the warmth of her covering, but perhaps if she didn't fight, she would relax into sleep easier.

He raised her to rest against his shoulder and rubbed her back as Elise had done so many times. He couldn't hum the way she did, but perhaps simply talking to his daughter in a steady voice would help.

"It's time to go to sleep, my little one. You'll feel much better when you wake." His mind could find nothing more to say, unless he told her of his frustrations. But he couldn't do that.

Perhaps he could speak with God as he walked, ask for His help to protect these children—*before* something bad happened to them, not at the last possible moment.

He cleared his throat so he could speak quietly. "God who created this daughter, protect her. Strengthen her limbs and give her the peace to sleep. Keep her safe from enemies, from poisons, from everything I can't protect her from. Let her life be filled with smiles and good things."

Pretty Shield stopped squirming and lay quietly on his shoulder. He'd slowed his walk to almost a crawl. Did he have to keep speaking for her to rest? His mind needed quiet, needed time in the near darkness with the wind gusting around him for the fury of nature to wipe away the mire of his thoughts.

Another flash of light and blast of thunder came at nearly the same moment, and much closer than the others. His daughter jerked in his arms, but he tightened his hold so she could feel his steadiness.

Large drops of rain splattered on his buckskins, a few splashing his face. He adjusted Pretty Shield's covering so she wouldn't get wet. The fur would keep the water from seeping through to the blanket.

He didn't mind getting wet himself. It would be a welcome discomfort, something familiar he could distract himself with.

As the rain began to fall steadily, Pretty Shield lay still against his shoulder. He checked twice to make sure breathing air could reach her, and the second time, her eyes had closed. Not even the thunder booms awakened her.

He needed to return to camp now. He should be with Walking Bird during the storm. A flash of frustration pressed through him. He'd forgotten the boy had feared so last time. He couldn't remember Walking Bird being afraid of storms in the past, but maybe something had happened to him with the Sioux. Just when Goes Ahead was beginning to feel like a better father, he forgot something important like that.

He turned to his backtrail and lengthened his stride, though he still tried to keep his steps steady so his daughter didn't awaken. By the time he reached camp, darkness had fallen in earnest, but with the rain, he couldn't see the campfire until he'd nearly stepped into the circle of light. The noise from the pounding of the drops on the oilskin they'd stretched over the fire grew louder as he stopped at the edge of the cover.

Ben was lighting a lantern from the leaping flames, and his face jerked up when Goes Ahead stepped into view. "Oh good. Glad you're back. Did Walking Bird find you?"

All Goes Ahead's senses leapt to alert. "No." He looked to the pallet where he'd left Walking Bird.

Empty.

"Where is my son?" He worked to keep himself from showing worry as he scanned the rest of the camp. Empty except for Ben. A fist clenched in his belly. His son. Had they lost him?

Ben closed the lantern and stood, then stepped nearer to Goes Ahead. The worry marking his face deepened. "He disappeared."

CHAPTER 18

*G*oes Ahead ignored the panic welling inside him and honed in on every word Ben said.

"Walking Bird was sitting on his bed, then we turned around and he was gone. I thought maybe he'd gone to relieve himself, but we couldn't find him. So then we thought he went after you. My sister and White Owl and Lola have gone out to search again. I came back to get this lantern and see if I could find you."

Goes Ahead spun but stopped himself from charging out into the rain. He needed to have his hands free, but he couldn't lay his daughter down and leave her. He'd have to carry her with him.

He also had to keep a clear head. Moving toward Walking Bird's bedding, he studied the ground in the light of the fire. "Do you know which way he went?" There were too many prints here since they'd wiped the snow away from this spot. Not even he could tell which were his son's.

"We didn't see him leave."

Goes Ahead scanned both of the paths that led out of camp. Under the oilskin, so many tracks had been stamped in the

147

mud, it would take time to decipher them. Time he couldn't spend.

Had Walking Bird waited until the others weren't looking to sneak away? And why weren't they looking? Hadn't Lola promised she would watch him carefully?

But he couldn't dwell on those thoughts now. He had to keep his focus on finding his boy.

If Walking Bird waited until no one watched to sneak away, he might have crept through the bushes behind his sleeping area.

Two strides brought Goes Ahead to the place, and he crouched low, peering over his daughter to see the ground.

There. Small moccasin tracks disappeared into the brush.

He leaned forward and parted the thick needled branches. Surely he would see a pair of eyes staring back at him.

But beyond the branches lay open space. Or rather the rising slope of the mountain they camped beside. "Walking Bird!"

No answer from the boy.

Goes Ahead pushed up to his feet, then moved around the shrubby trees to reach the other side. With no shelter over this area, the rain had washed away any sign of his son's footprints.

In the distance, a little ways up the slope, a figure caught his gaze.

Elise moved quickly, peering around low trees and rocks as she made her way uphill at an angle. His heartbeat quickened as it did every time he saw her, though now it was probably only fear for his son.

He turned a slow circle, searching out every shadow on the slope with his gaze. Why would Walking Bird have left the camp? He'd promised to stay.

It made sense that he might have tried to follow Goes Ahead, though he'd seen nothing of his son as he retraced his steps back to camp. Maybe the boy had gotten off course.

He started the direction he'd gone earlier, lifting his voice to yell out for Walking Bird. The rain drowned out most of the sound, then a fierce clap of thunder overwhelmed even the echo of his thoughts.

The boy's new fear of storms... He must be terrified. Had he found a place to hide from the noise and rain? It might take until the storm passed to find him, and that could be well into the night.

They had to find him.

Goes Ahead couldn't let this panic overwhelm him. He had to think straight. Had to save his son from this danger that could not only hurt his body but bring terror to his mind.

As he wove through trees and around boulders, searching low and high, he had to move slower than usual because he still carried his daughter. Pretty Shield hadn't made a sound, or if she had, he'd not heard it over the storm. He did his best to keep her dry, though water ran down his own face and had long ago soaked his leathers.

He took a route just beside the path he'd traveled before, but he reached the point where he'd turned around, finding no sign of his son.

He tried to fight the images that flooded his mind—the boy curled into a ball, drenched and so scared he trembled. Or maybe he'd slipped on the wet rocks and broken an arm, or perhaps a leg. That might be why he hadn't returned to camp. Or worse, maybe he'd struck his head and even now lay like the sleep of the dead. Or even truly dead.

He couldn't give over to those thoughts. A warrior kept his focus fully honed.

He moved farther down the slope to the other side of the path he'd first taken to soothe his daughter to sleep.

After only a few steps, the howling wind spoke his name. He spun to find the source.

The wind couldn't be calling him.

A glimpse of light-colored fabric made his heart race. But

the figure wasn't his son. Elise ran down the mountainside toward him, slipping in the steeper places and grabbing branches and rocks to slow her descent. Had she found the boy? Maybe she needed help carrying him.

As another flash lit the air around them, he started toward her, running up the slope and leaping over rocks as best he could without risking his daughter.

When he reached Elise, she grabbed his arm and nearly collapsed against him as she struggled for breath.

"What's wrong? Did you find him? Is he hurt?"

She shook her head but still struggled to catch enough breath to speak.

He gripped her shoulder, willing her to tell him what she'd found.

When she finally lifted her face to him, her eyes showed red, even in the darkness. Rain pressed her hair flat to her head and cheeks.

At last, her throat worked and she opened her mouth to speak. "We need to pray."

The words were so far from what he'd expected, his frantic mind stuttered to make sense of them. Where was his son? What had she found?

But then her meaning sank in. They needed the great God to show them.

Yes.

The wash of certainty—almost relief—that flooded his chest made him straighten. He studied Elise's face. "Will you pray?" He'd never felt so unable, not even during those nights when he'd held his hungry crying daughter.

The fear twisting Elise's face, the clear evidence she'd been crying, meant she might feel just as helpless. But she closed her eyes.

Keeping one hand on his arm, she placed the other on the fur that covered Pretty Shield, wrapping them both in her petition. "Father. God who sees all. Creator who made Walking Bird and loves him more deeply even than we do. Show us where he is. Guide us to the place, and help us help him. Let Your power be revealed for all to see, and teach us all what You would have us learn through this trial. Give us Your peace so we can rest in Your strength and never-ending love. In Jesus name, we lift this petition to You. Amen."

He didn't understand every word she prayed, though a few had come clear in his mind, raising up thoughts and ideas he would examine. Later.

But for now, a strange sort of peace cleared away the muddle in his thoughts. Maybe the peace Elise had just prayed for.

And two thoughts resounded inside him. Elise was a woman above others, with a depth of heart and strength he'd rarely seen, even among warriors.

And she loved his son with that same strength. He'd heard it in her voice, felt it in the tenderness of her touch, in the air around her. He could trust her to act in that love, to do everything she could for Walking Bird—to find him, to help him, to protect him.

When she opened her eyes, he realized he'd not closed his own. That custom still seemed odd to him when speaking to the great God.

For a moment, they simply looked at each other. Her eyes said she was working through something in her thoughts.

His own moment of clear thinking seemed to have fled, pushed out by the cloud that took over his mind. So he waited for her. He had to start looking for his son again, but first he would hear whether God had shown Elise where they should search.

Her brow formed lines. Another clap of thunder boomed around them, but Elise didn't seem to hear it. As soon as the noise faded, she spoke above the rain. "I keep seeing a picture of water. Like a small river or stream."

Certainty pressed in on him, and he spun to study the slope of the land. There was a stream down the slope toward the opposite side of the mountain. Why would Walking Bird go there?

Elise's hand pulled away from his arm, then her fingers touched his hand, and her palm settled against his own. He tightened his grip around hers and started forward.

He moved as fast as he dared on the wet rocks with his daughter in his arms. Elise stayed with him, at his side but slightly behind to avoid branches and rocks in the path. She didn't slow him down. If anything, her hand in his made his steps steadier, keeping him from sliding at times.

In the dark and with so much rain, he couldn't determine how far away the creek was, but they ran in the right direction. They had to reach it soon.

Images tried to rise of what might have happened to his son in the water, but he pushed them aside. A tug on his shoulder grabbed his attention, and he slowed enough to look over.

Elise pointed, and he followed the line of her finger to two figures approaching through the curtain of rain. Had the downpour grown stronger?

White Owl and Lola ran toward them, the woman carrying a bundle that must be her own daughter.

His heart picked up speed even as he slowed to meet them. Had they found something?

When they came near enough to be heard above the storm, Elise called out, "Have you seen Walking Bird?"

Lola shook her head, and as they met, White Owl motioned to the mountain behind them. "We searched on this side of the camp as far up as he could've gone."

Lola struggled for breath as Elise had done. "Ben went down to look in the valley and check the creek. We were coming to help him."

The creek. Had God spoken the same message to them all?

Goes Ahead turned back that direction. "We are going to the water also."

"We'll follow you." Lola waved them forward.

He led the way through the pouring rain, trying to keep them pointed down the slope at an angle, though sometimes clusters of rocks made them go uphill for a distance before turning downward again.

At last, they reached level ground, and through the haze of rain and darkness appeared a line of trees that marked the creek. The pounding of his blood through his ears rose even above the sounds of the storm.

Another flash lit the land around them, illuminating a figure at the edge of the trees. The form held something small and glowing.

Ben with the lantern.

Goes Ahead surged toward him, running now. Maybe too fast, for Elise jerked hard on his hand. He slowed enough to glance back at her.

"Let me take the baby." She pointed to Pretty Shield as she yelled loudly enough to be heard.

He halted just long enough to hand over the precious bundle. Elise would protect her, and his arms would be free to find his son.

As she took the babe in both hands, tucking her close, her gaze held his for a heartbeat. "God will help you." The words seemed as much inside his own mind as spoken in her voice.

They gave him a new strength as he turned and sprinted toward the place Ben had stood. The trees must be hiding him now. Had he found Walking Bird?

When Goes Ahead reached the line of brush, he had to slow and push aside branches to step through. White Owl came just behind him.

"Over here!"

Goes Ahead followed Ben's voice, and the light finally

appeared upstream. The sound of the rain had dimmed under the canopy of branches, but the echo of rushing water soon rose above it. This had been a simple creek earlier, but the rainwater had turned the flow into a torrent.

He pushed aside vines and branches to finally reach the man, then he followed Ben's gaze into the water.

"I think that's him." The man panted with the effort of scrambling through the thick woods.

Even while Goes Ahead's eyes searched for the form of his son, his mind took in how the bank rose above the water's surface in this place. The current surged fast enough to form foam he could see even from this distance in the dark.

There. His chest seized. He'd first thought the spot was a rock but... The movement drew his focus back to the place.

Walking Bird. Only the top half of his body showed, lying on a stone above the water.

Was he alive?

CHAPTER 19

*G*oes Ahead stepped forward to dive into the water and swim to his son, but a hand gripped his arm.

"Wait!" Ben yelled over the river's roaring. "I don't think the water is deep enough to jump. The bank's too high up. Let yourself down from the edge. We can help lower you."

The pause stopped him long enough to see the man was right. But the distance from the top of the bank to the water's surface looked barely taller than the length of his body. He could drop from there.

Slipping down to his belly at the edge, he turned and let his feet hang over the river, then he lowered himself until only his hands gripped the ground above. He pushed himself away from the bank as he let go.

His moccasins hit the water, then sank down into the icy liquid until his feet finally found something solid. One foot landed on a stone, and his ankle bent as the stone shifted beneath him. He scrambled to stay upright, bracing his hands on the rock wall beside him until he caught his balance. The water came up nearly to the tops of his legs, and its frigid clutches wrapped around him.

He had to get to Walking Bird.

He turned and slogged through the water, pushing hard to fight the current that tried to sweep him sideways.

He could see his son better now, but he still couldn't tell if he was alive. The boy lay on a rock—whether clutching or resting, he couldn't tell—with his face turned away.

But when Goes Ahead only had a few steps left to reach him, Walking Bird lifted his head. Relief swept through him, easing some of the weight from his chest. His son was alive. He pushed harder to reach him.

"Father!"

He could barely hear the rasping voice over the rushing water, but one more step brought him to his side.

He reached down and gripped Walking Bird's arms, near his shoulders. He'd never been so thankful to feel that bony flesh. Though his eyes burned with the love pulsing through him, he ⁻lifted Walking Bird up from the water. His body felt heavier than usual.

The boy cried out, and he gripped Goes Ahead's hair with a hard pull.

Part of the boy still hung in the water, but Goes Ahead stilled.

"My foot!" Walking Bird screamed and pushed against Goes Ahead's chest.

The foot must be stuck under a rock.

Goes Ahead eased his son back down and shifted so he could hold him around the chest with one arm while he released the leg.

He found the knee in the water, then ran his hand down to locate the part caught by the stone. His hand struck icy rock just below the knee. He tried to work the leg free, but it seemed caught under two rocks where they met. Heavy stones that couldn't be moved with one hand. Especially not with the weight of the water pressing down on them. One of them must be the boulder Walking Bird had been clinging to.

He gripped the leg and tried to wiggle it free.

"Argg!" Walking Bird's cry stilled his efforts. A little bit of pain would be worth getting him out of this icy water, but he didn't want to break the bone unless there was no other way to free him.

"How is he caught?" Ben's voice sounded behind him.

He'd come to help. *Thank you, Creator Father.*

"Foot stuck under rock." Goes Ahead shifted so he could hand his son to the man. "Hold him while I lift the stone. Keep him low so you don't hurt the leg."

As he handed Walking Bird's nearly-limp body to Ben, a tremble shook the child. *Help him.* He'd barely recovered from the poison. How long had he lain in this icy water?

And why had he come to this place? That question would have to be answered later.

With his hands free, Goes Ahead reached deep and found the boy's knee again, then used his fingers to circle his leg where it met the rocks. If he could simply turn the limb enough to free the foot, that would be easiest. But these boulders were pressed too tight against him. Goes Ahead would have to lift them off.

He felt the stones to see which lay on top. The one that rose up out of the water. The one Walking Bird had been clutching. From what he could tell, it was the largest one.

He positioned his hands where he could grip, though it was hard to get more than a fingertip hold on the curved edges. With a heave, he lifted. The rock shifted, and he strained harder.

But the stone wouldn't move any farther, as though something else pressed it down.

"I will help." White Owl waded through the water and positioned himself on the other end of the stone.

"There are two on his leg." Goes Ahead nodded toward the

rock rising above the water's surface. "If we get this big one off, he may be free."

White Owl placed his hands on the part of the rock he could see and ran them down into the water as he searched for a grip. Only then did Goes Ahead realize he'd spoken in Atsina. But the man seemed to understand.

When White Owl nodded that he'd found a place to hold, Goes Ahead wrapped his fingers around the base of the stone. "Lift!"

He put all his strength into the effort, but the boulder barely moved. They wouldn't be able to raise it. They would have to shift it to the side. White Owl seemed to realize that also and shifted his angle. Had they lifted enough to pull Walking Bird's foot out? He couldn't free a hand to reach for the leg, but he managed to grunt, "Free leg?"

White Owl barked something to Ben. Goes Ahead must have spoken Atsina again and he was interpreting, though his words came as hard as Goes Ahead's own.

Ben reached down. His arm brushed Goes Ahead's as he tried to pull the leg free.

The boy's scream of pain rose so loud, Goes Ahead's fingers slipped on the stone. It took everything he had not to drop the boulder.

"Lift more!" He pushed his body into the effort, bracing his feet on the creek's rocky floor. Every part of him heaved, his neck and head expanding like they might explode.

The stone moved. They couldn't stop. Not until his son was free.

The smallest bit at a time, the boulder shifted over. Something seemed to be pushing just as hard against them, but surely they'd almost done it.

Gray surrounded his vision, making it harder to keep up his strength. The gray turned to black, closing tighter, narrowing his sight to a small circle.

No. This couldn't happen now. Not until his son was safe. *Great God, I need You now more than I ever have before. Take over where my strength is not enough.*

The rock moved again, more this time. A shout rang out beside him, but that small circle of vision had narrowed to the tip of an arrow. He couldn't last much longer.

"He's free! You can let go."

The words reached him through the haze. But his body obeyed, understanding what his mind could not. He slumped down, his cheek landing on the rock where Walking Bird's had first rested. His eyes closed, but his mind began to clear.

They'd done it. That desperate prayer had been the turning point. The great God had been the One to free his son.

Thank You.

≈

E lise could barely breathe as she lay on the bank watching. Walking Bird was free.

She'd thrust Pretty Shield into Lola's arm so she could climb down and help rescue the boy, but Lola had stopped her just in time. *They'll need you up here so they can lift him up to you.*

She was right. Lola had a gift for thinking ahead like that.

But she'd felt so helpless when the men worked while she lay there doing nothing. Walking Bird's screams of pain had pierced her in a hundred places. She squeezed her eyes shut to block the sounds from her memory.

Goes Ahead held him close now as they turned toward her. The tiny sounds of the boy's voice barely reached her, but as Goes Ahead dipped his head to speak to his son, her eyes caught on the leg that had been pinned.

Walking Bird held it stiff. He pointed toward the foot as he spoke to his father, and his whimpers squeezed her chest.

As Goes Ahead placed a hand under the calf and lifted, the

boy ducked his face into his father's neck and wrapped his arms around him. Hiding from the pain.

Lord, don't let the leg be broken.

Walking Bird had been through so much—the kidnapping, his mother's death, leaving his home, the poison berries. And now this. Did he really have to have a broken leg too?

She squeezed her eyes shut. *God, when is it enough? Why must he suffer even more?*

A thought crept in. Or rather, a Scripture. *But we glory in tribulations also, knowing that tribulation worketh patience.* She savored the familiar verse. What came after patience? *And patience, experience; and experience, hope.*

Hope. Was God saying these trials were given to the boy to develop him? To give him a future full of hope? Something else came after that passage. She couldn't recall the exact words, but they said something about that hope not leading to disappointment, but that the trials show how much God loves us because He gives us His Holy Spirit. *Lord, use these awful things to show Walking Bird how much You love him. Draw Him to You so he can experience the help of the Holy Spirit.*

God loved this precious boy even more than she did. She had to trust He was creating good in Walking Bird through them all.

Goes Ahead had nearly reached the cliff wall beneath her, and she reached down with both hands. "Can you lift him up to me?"

He studied her, and she could see the apprehension in his eyes. Would he trust her with his boy? She could understand if he didn't want to release him.

He dipped his head to murmur something to his son. Walking Bird loosened his arms from his father's neck, then Goes Ahead lifted him up above his head.

Lying on the bank with her arms extended over the edge, she

gripped the lad around his chest. His bony body felt so frail beneath her hands. When she had a tight hold, she lifted him up.

As soon as he was close enough, he flung his arms around her neck. She hauled him up onto the bank, then struggled up to a sitting position and pulled him onto her lap.

She wrapped her arms all the way around him, soaking in the scent of little boy she'd come to love so much. "Oh, Walking Bird. My boy. You're safe now." He clung to her, and she rocked him back and forth, murmuring in his ear. "You're safe and loved. God loves you. I love you. Your Papa loves you. Your sister loves you. We all love our Walking Bird." Someone had laid a fur over him, but she couldn't see who through the tears clouding her eyes. She'd never known it was possible to feel so broken, yet so whole at the same time.

Strong arms came around her, one behind her back and one encircling Walking Bird. She leaned into Goes Ahead's side, resting her head against his shoulder, soaking in the strength of a man she knew far better than she'd allowed herself to believe.

She might not know all the details of his past, but that would come. What she did know was his present. She'd seen his heart with these children over and over. She'd seen him seeking, though he didn't always realize it was a Strength greater than his own he sought. She'd helped him meet his Creator and watched him learn and press deeper into his new faith. As they'd prayed together on the mountainside during the desperate search for Walking Bird, a certainty had surged through her. This is what God intended for her. This man. And this sweet boy and girl.

Her spirit had realized that truth early on, but she'd been thinking through the details from a human perspective. Joining with this man didn't make sense to others, but if God had planned Goes Ahead for her, their union would be blessed.

She nestled deeper against him, and he tightened his grip

around her. She would be content to live by this man's side for the rest of her days.

CHAPTER 20

*I*f only Elise could have a few minutes alone to talk with Goes Ahead. So much had happened that day, especially all the work necessary to care for Walking Bird's broken leg. The bone ends hadn't pierced the skin, but the swelling and angle of the limb made a break seem likely. Ben had splinted the leg by the light of the fire while Goes Ahead held his son still.

Walking Bird's cries had been awful, and when Elise couldn't bear them anymore, she looked away. But her gaze had caught on Goes Ahead's face. A glimmer of liquid slid down one cheek. His jaw was set hard, but the awfulness of what he had to do—after everything his son had already suffered—must be tearing his insides apart.

At last, the boy had fallen asleep, then the rest of them finally collapsed into weary rest while the rain pounded on the oilskins above them. At least the lightning and thunder had stopped.

This morning had come too soon, beginning with Walking Bird's whimpers, which had awakened his sister. Pretty Shield's hungry cries soon roused them all, including little Anna, who

MISTY M. BELLER

was also eager to break her fast. Poor Lola had her hands full, no matter how much Elise tried to help.

They'd finally pulled enough answers from Walking Bird to understand why he'd left the camp the night before. The reason still made tears well in her eyes every time she thought of it.

With his sister so fussy, he'd gone to find a rabbit so he could bring her a fresh fur. That precious boy had remembered their conversation from days before, had seen how restless she was, and had wanted to be a brave warrior just like his papa. He'd slipped away from camp and headed down the slope, which must have been the easiest direction for him to take. He must have scared a rabbit from the brush, then chased it to new cover in the trees beside the river. Somehow he'd slipped into the water and been caught in the current.

Until that rock snagged his leg.

If the stone hadn't caught him and given him support to keep his head above the surface, would he have drowned? She pressed her eyes shut. *Lord, thank You for saving our precious boy.*

He was finally sleeping now that the morning had nearly passed. All three children slept, in fact—and Lola too. They should all be exhausted enough to slumber for quite a while.

Elise and the men sat at the fire, attending to small jobs that had been put off while they traveled. She had a stack of mending to do. Mostly tears in her brother's clothing, but one of Walking Bird's beautiful tunics had been ripped by a branch while they rode. Hopefully, she could restore it as well as Bright Eyes would have.

A stack of freshly-sharpened knives sat beside White Owl— all the hunting blades the men carried, as well as the carving knife she and Lola used for cooking.

Ben had just finished cleaning and greasing the straps on their saddles and bridles, removing all the mud caked from so many days riding through snow and slush.

And Goes Ahead... He'd pulled out a stack of sticks he must

have been saving to whittle into arrows, and though his fingers worked steadily, stripping the bark and shaving off bumps, the V of his brows indicated that his mind had drifted far away. What thoughts troubled him so? She could think of a hundred things that could bring on a look like that, but her heart longed to know *exactly* what swirled within him.

Maybe he felt her gaze, for he turned to her. As their eyes met for a heartbeat, the line of his mouth softened into almost a smile. Every part of her wanted to reach out and touch him. To tell him what she'd realized during the horror of last night's events.

But she couldn't do so in front of Ben and White Owl. Did she dare ask Goes Ahead to walk with her? It would bring on questions from her brother, for certain. Questions she would gladly answer, but not until she'd talked to Goes Ahead.

Ben set aside a bridle. "Guess I'll bring up more firewood. We need to dry out a bunch of it after the rain last night."

Her heart lifted. With Ben gone, maybe she could work up the nerve to pull Goes Ahead aside. It shouldn't matter to her what her brother thought. But it did, just a little. If only he could be pleased with her choices. Be happy for her and encourage herself and Goes Ahead in this union. They would likely face plenty of challenges, not just the difficulties of uniting two into one, but the displeasure and even prejudice of so many from both cultures. It would make things a little easier if she had the support of her family.

But even if Ben staunchly opposed this decision, the peace within her had become even stronger today. God had chosen Goes Ahead for her. Had created her for him. He would give them strength for whatever lay ahead.

As Ben disappeared down the slope toward the trees where they'd been gathering wood, White Owl moved to the supplies and placed each knife in its place. He glanced at his sleeping wife and daughter. "I go to check the horses. They will need new grazing, I think."

She should offer to help. Moving all the animals could be a challenging job for one person.

As White Owl stood, he glanced back at her and Goes Ahead. "You will stay here in case they awaken?" His gaze darted to the sleeping forms again.

A weight lifted from her chest. "We'll be here." She shot a look at Goes Ahead. Perhaps she shouldn't have spoken for him.

But he dipped his chin also. White Owl returned the gesture, then set off on the path toward the animals.

At last, she and Goes Ahead were alone, if one didn't count those stretched out under furs and breathing steadily. Surely none of them would hear their conversation.

Goes Ahead's dark gaze was already on her, though his expression was hard to read. It wasn't swimming with love as she'd have hoped. Nay, his eyes seemed more guarded. And why wouldn't they be? She'd told him they were too different. That the two of them together could never work.

She swallowed and took in a breath for courage. "Goes Ahead, I need to tell you that I was wrong."

He gave no reaction, so she pressed forward.

"When I told you we were too different, I think I was afraid. Afraid of what I didn't know. Afraid of how hard it would be. But last night, I realized my fear doesn't matter. God brought us together for a reason, and He'll give me the courage and strength to face whatever comes. I can't imagine losing you and your two precious ones." She pressed a hand to her chest and fought the burn in her eyes. "The three of you have taken over my heart. If it's not too late…"

He still said nothing, and she couldn't bring herself to finish that thought. Not without any sign of whether he also felt the same.

Holding his gaze took every bit of courage she had left, especially when the intensity of his eyes deepened. His focus stayed locked with hers as he rose to his feet. She had to crane her neck to watch him, but she couldn't look away. Her chest could barely push air in and out.

He stepped to her and reached out a hand. The action didn't seem an offering of peace.

It felt more like a choice—she could stay protected in the comfortable world she knew, or take his hand and step out in faith.

Faith that God really had the best planned for her, no matter how hard the journey might be, and faith that He would be there through every challenge.

Faith that Goes Ahead was the man she'd come to know as she'd seen his character through every obstacle they'd faced on this journey.

Faith that they could grow together. That by his side, life would not only be manageable, but wonderful. Full of joy and passion and a host of amazements she would never discover if she stayed confined to what she knew.

Faith in all of that and so much more radiated in her being.

She slid her palm against his hand.

He tightened his grip around hers, pulling her up with a strength that made the act seem easy. His tug didn't stop when she reached her feet, but he drew her to himself, wrapping his arms around her back. She placed her hands on his chest, settling one directly over his heart. The thumping beneath her palm proved just how alive he was. Its rhythm swept through her own being, awakening a sensation inside her that tasted like excitement.

She couldn't break away from his gaze, though she could read it a little better now. And the emotion shimmering in those dark pools looked so much like hope, her chest ached. Could he really still want her after everything?

When he finally spoke, his voice rumbled deeper than usual. "I did not know how I would let you go. I asked the great God to help me. To give me the strength to accept what you said." One of his hands came up from her back, and his fingers cupped her cheek. Their rough surface was just one more reminder of his strength. Strength she was growing to love more and more —along with everything else about him.

She leaned into his hand, and a twinkle lit his eyes. His lips twitched before he spoke. "I like the way our God answered what I asked."

His gaze dropped to her lips, and she lost the last of her ability to breathe as she anticipated the touch of his mouth.

The warmth of his breath reached her just before his lips brushed over hers. His mouth stroked hers in a single exquisite caress that nearly stole the strength from her knees.

He pulled back, and her throat made a squeak as her body ached with the loss of his touch. But he rested his forehead on her brow, pulling her even closer with his hand on her back. She sank into the warm security of his hold.

"This that I feel for you is stronger than anything I have known before." The murmur of his voice wrapped her in a delicious warmth. "As long as I have strength in my body..." His voice slowed, took on a tone even more certain. "...and with the strength of Creator Father, I will always protect you. I will make sure you want nothing. Not food. Not warmth. And most of all, not my arms around you and all that I hold inside me. I will learn the ways of your people. How to live in the white man's world." His eyes crinkled. "I will be happy to learn how it is to have so many brothers and sisters."

A jolt slipped through her as realization settled in. "I... You want to come back to the States with me? To Marcyville?" Her mind had been forming a very different future.

Hesitation flickered across his face. "With the White Clay

People, it is the custom for the warrior to join the clan of his woman. Is this not the way with the white man?"

She nibbled the inside of her lip. "I suppose it is most of the time, though not always." Did she dare say what she'd been thinking? She had to get used to speaking even hard things with him.

He was watching her, and he raised his brows. "But this is not what you want?"

A weight lifted from her, and she let her mouth creep up in a smile. "I have an idea."

CHAPTER 21

*B*en had been watching Goes Ahead as the sun moved down its path to the tops of the mountains, as though he knew something had changed between him and Elise.

Maybe the lightness that lifted Goes Ahead's chest also showed on his face. And perhaps the fact that he couldn't keep his gaze from moving to Elise had caught her brother's notice. Everything she did made the feelings inside him grow stronger. The graceful way she held herself as she worked over the fire, cooking a special stew for Walking Bird to help with his pain and heal the bone. The love in every touch as she snuggled beside the boy and talked with him while he ate. His son had been through so many hard things, but with Elise and Creator Father helping him heal, he would come out of this journey stronger than ever before—both in body and spirit.

She spoke to his son of Creator Father, too, something Goes Ahead hadn't done as much as he should. The words seemed to come so easily for Elise, a part of her nature. No wonder the great God had called her to come to this place to tell the tribes of His love.

His gaze shifted to Ben. The two of them sat at the fire that lit their camp this night. Lola and White Owl had already stretched out in their furs, since she'd seemed especially tired as the darkness settled over the land. White Owl had watched her with concern marking his brow. This journey had been hard on Lola, yet she never complained about the challenges of feeding both babes.

Goes Ahead could never bring her enough horses or fine furs to thank her for providing life to his daughter, but he would find a way to show his thanks when they reached his father's village.

And that thought sent his focus back to Ben.

The man watched him, his mood hard to decipher. Not as much wariness or distrust, which had once shown in his expression when he looked at Goes Ahead. But this wasn't friendliness either.

Could now be the right time to speak with him?

Goes Ahead glanced at Elise, who was snuggling Walking Bird on the boy's bed pallet. His son had stopped eating and leaned into her side as she spoke. Her words were too soft to reach across the distance, but from the way Walking Bird listened, she must be telling a story. Or perhaps singing?

He could watch them all night, but the weight of Ben's gaze pressed in on him. When he glanced back at Elise's brother, Ben lifted his brows. "Want to walk with me to check the horses? The new pasture White Owl took them to gives them room to roam, so might be good to make sure they're staying close."

Did the man also wish to speak his own words to Goes Ahead? It was time they talk clearly with each other.

The path was wide enough for them to walk side by side, and their breath clouded as they maneuvered the rocky ground. The clear call of the night sounds eased his spirit, though soon enough the noises faded into the crunching of grazing horses.

His eyes swept the forms of the animals to make sure all

were there and seemed healthy. Then his focus honed on his stallion. The horse ate as the others did, and in the light of the small moon, he looked to have fully recovered from the poison berries. That seemed so long ago, though it had only been two sleeps.

They slowed as they approached the animals, and Ben motioned to the stallion. "He seems much better. It's good there's plenty of grass here so the animals can fatten up some while we wait."

All of the horses had grown lean as they crossed the mountains, but that was to be expected through the snowy moons. But Ben's comment raised another question, one none of their group had voiced aloud yet. "I do not know when my son will be ready to ride again." In the past, he wouldn't have spoken that he didn't know something. He would have found a way to get Ben to give his opinion without admitting his own lack. But on this journey, he'd had to face how unable he was in so many ways, with his children especially. None of these people had looked down on him for being incapable. And they didn't hesitate to speak of their own flaws either.

Ben held his tongue for several breaths, then he shook his head. "I don't know either. I suppose we should take one day at a time. See how Walking Bird feels. The splint will help protect the leg, but we don't want to wear him out."

He looked at Goes Ahead. "Do you think our camping spot will suit for a few more days, or should we look for something closer to water and more firewood?"

As his mind worked through the best answer to the question, he realized the honor the man paid him by asking. Goes Ahead had been leading most of their trek, but he wasn't truly in charge. They were on this journey together. They needed everyone's efforts and wisdom and abilities to reach the other side of the mountains safely.

"It will be harder to move than to carry what we need to the place we camp now."

Ben turned his gaze toward the animals again. "I suppose it would be hard on the little ones to move."

Silence settled over them again, which meant this was his time to speak. *Great Father, make my words sweet in his ears.*

He looked over at the man, and Ben met his gaze with lifted brows. He gathered the English words he'd planned out. "When we first met at the place of death, you said you did not know where you and your sister would go next. What village you would stay in to tell the people of Creator Father."

Ben dipped his chin in a slow nod. "That's right."

"I ask that you come to my father's village. That you stay there and help me tell them of the great God. The One who made the land and the people. The One who wishes them to know Him as Father." While he watched Ben's face for his response, he sent up another prayer for favor.

The night shadows hid most of his thoughts, but the lines that deepened his brow showed much passed through his mind.

At last, he spoke. "I had thought about that. It seems like a good idea in many ways. The people will be more open to us with you there. And you can help interpret our words." He paused for a heartbeat. "I guess I need to speak plain. I know you and my sister have...well, there's something sparking between you two. You might have realized I was struggling with what I saw growing there. She's spoken to me a little about you, and I told her I thought the two of you would have too many challenges, coming from different cultures as you do."

The knot in his belly clenched tighter. Ben hadn't changed his mind then. What could Goes Ahead do to convince him?

But Ben wasn't finished. "Since then, I've been watching you. Both of you, I mean. And I've been praying a lot about it." Ben turned his body to face him, and his voice turned earnest. "I see how much my sister loves you, and it seems there's an awful lot of the same on your side."

He paused. Probably waiting for Goes Ahead to agree or not. But he'd barely sorted an answer in his mind when Ben continued. "Love alone wouldn't be enough though, because I know feelings can change. But I've also seen the strength of your character, how well you care for those important to you. On top of that, the Lord's given me something of a peace about the situation." He raised his hand, though Goes Ahead wouldn't have been sure of his words if given the opportunity to speak. "I still think you should take a while to get to know each other better before you decide for certain."

Then he lowered his hand, and the corners of his mouth tugged up. "If we stay with your village for a while, that might be just the time the two of you need. Then, if Elise is willing, I'd be honored to call you my brother in that way too."

The relief that swept through Goes Ahead's chest took away the remaining weight that had pressed down on him. The lightness left room for something he'd not felt in so long...joy, which filled up the last of the spaces that had held only pain for so long. "This is a good plan."

But the happiness swirling inside wouldn't be constrained. He turned to Ben and grinned.

EPILOGUE

*E*lise didn't have to touch Goes Ahead to feel the tension coiled impossibly thick inside him as he rode ahead of their group toward the cluster of lodges. Which structure belonged to his parents?

He'd scouted the area for several days to find this camp, and once he'd seen from a distance that his father was there, he'd come back to retrieve the rest of them. The fact that he hadn't approached the village when he'd first found them told her much about how nervous he was to meet his family again.

But his words had told her even more. The two of them had begun taking Walking Bird and Pretty Shield for a walk in the evenings after they set up camp. While the boy played, throwing rocks in the river or gathering small branches for the fire, she and Goes Ahead talked. He didn't seem to mind her many questions about life growing up among the White Clay People. The stories he told gave her a wonderful glimpse of those who had helped develop him into the man he was today. How many of those friends would still live in this village now?

Ahead of them, a group of children playing outside of camp stopped to watch their approach. A few figures moved among the lodges, and two men stepped out of the village toward them. She glanced at Goes Ahead, who was studying the newcomers intently. They were near enough that he would recognize them if he knew them, wouldn't he? Surely the people hadn't changed so much in the five years he'd been gone.

When their group came within speaking distance of the men, Goes Ahead halted. Walking Bird rode behind his father. The splint on his leg kept him more comfortable on horseback than Elise would have expected. Pretty Shield slept in the sling at her chest, and she stopped her horse just behind Goes Ahead's stallion. Ben halted beside her, and White Owl and Lola reined in on her other side.

Goes Ahead spoke to the men in their tongue—Atsina, he called the language. And after only a few words, the men's expressions shifted from wary to something like surprise or even pleasure. They spoke as well, the words sounding like a question.

Goes Ahead's gaze flicked to the lodges beyond as he answered. Then one of the men turned and called out to someone within the village. A small group had gathered just inside the first row of teepees, and the man's words started a murmur among them. One youngster split off from those talking and ran deeper among the structures.

She shifted her focus to the warrior sitting tall on his stallion beside her. If only she could reach out and place a hand on his arm, maybe weave her fingers between his to show he didn't have to face this meeting alone. But he knew she was there. They'd talked about it that morning, when he'd voiced his worry about whether his mother still lived and how his father would receive him. It seemed words had been spoken between them at Goes Ahead's parting that he now grieved over.

When he'd told her that his father had worried over how his leaving would affect his mother, his voice had grown rough. The pain had shimmered in his eyes, and the urge to comfort him had made her step into his arms, wrapping her own around him and holding him tight.

If only she could do the same now.

As Goes Ahead studied the steadily-growing group gathered at the edge of the village, he straightened, and his demeanor shifted to something more akin to pleasure, though certainly suppressed. She followed his gaze to see who he was looking at, and the man who stepped from the crowd seemed just as excited as Goes Ahead. The brave appeared to be about his same age, though his face was rounder, and he might not be quite as tall.

The man walked right up to Goes Ahead's stallion, and Goes Ahead reached down so they could clasp arms. Conversation flowed freely between them, and as Goes Ahead spoke, he motioned back to Walking Bird, who'd tucked himself shyly behind his father. The other man spoke to the boy, and Walking Bird managed a few sounds in response, though he kept his cheek pressed to his father's back.

Then Goes Ahead turned to Elise and motioned for her to bring her horse forward. He pointed to Pretty Shield as he talked to his friend, and the man responded with a smile and nod as he answered.

Then Goes Ahead lifted his gaze to Elise and switched to English, but he kept his voice low to show he meant the words for her. "This is Catch the Wind."

She sucked in a breath. The friend who'd shot him with the poison arrow? During one of their walks with the children, he'd told her more details of the story, including how his parents had reacted. His poor mother. How much had losing all those children affected her? Elise could only imagine the depth of grief the woman had endured.

Goes Ahead gave the slightest of nods to show she'd remembered this friend's name correctly, then he turned to the man and spoke in Atsina as he motioned to her. Catch the Wind's eyes widened, and she glanced at Goes Ahead, then back to the man. What was he saying about her?

Then Goes Ahead turned to her and spoke softly in English again. "I told him you are the woman I wish to make my wife."

The heat rose up her neck and into her cheeks. She only managed a quick glance at Catch the Wind before returning her gaze to Goes Ahead—a much safer place to focus. She didn't want to know how this friend reacted to those words.

The corners of Goes Ahead's mouth tugged in the slightest of grins, but his eyes sparkled as he watched her. "If I do not make it clear from the beginning that you are taken, there will be a line of warriors outside your lodge trying to win your regard."

The heat in her cheeks turned to fire.

Thankfully, Goes Ahead shifted the conversation to introduce Ben and White Owl and Lola to his friend. As Catch the Wind responded with a greeting, Goes Ahead's attention snagged on something inside the village.

She followed his gaze to a woman standing just behind the group of people. Her gray hair hung loose in long scraggly strands, and she looked hunched and wrinkled enough to be his grandmother.

Goes Ahead started to bring his leg behind him to slide down from his horse, but realized just in time that his son sat behind him. He moved his leg in front then, but even as he held Walking Bird in place while he slid to the ground, his focus stayed riveted on the woman.

Her hand came up to her mouth as though trying to hold in words. Or maybe she couldn't believe what she was seeing.

Could this be his mother? Elise had pictured her younger, more her own mother's age. But he'd said nothing about a grandmother still living. Losing so many children—all her children in a way—could have aged her like this.

Ben had the presence of mind to dismount and grab Goes

Ahead's horse as he started forward. He seemed to be in such a trance that he might have left the stallion's rope to dangle, which wouldn't have been safe for his son.

She sent a quick glance to Walking Bird. He'd moved up to take his father's seat on the horse, back straight, putting on a brave front in the face of so many new people. But beneath his tough facade, he looked like the four-year-old boy he was.

Cradling Pretty Shield with one hand, Elise dismounted and moved around her gelding's head so she could stand beside Goes Ahead's son. Because of his splinted leg, she couldn't get him down without carrying him, but she reached up and placed a hand on his back so he wouldn't feel alone.

Then she turned her attention to Goes Ahead, walking slowly toward the older woman, who'd finally begun taking hobbling steps toward him. She wobbled as she progressed, like she needed a walking stick for balance. But no one came forward to help her. As bent as her shoulders were, she kept her eyes down as she walked.

But none of this stopped her from picking up speed as she left the lodges behind and aimed toward Goes Ahead. His stride lengthened, losing some of its hesitation.

When three steps separated them, he halted. The woman didn't stop though, just plowed forward, raising her arms just in time to fling them around Goes Ahead's middle. She came barely to the level of his heart, such a small frail woman clinging to a tall strapping brave.

He seemed stunned for a breath, then his hands came up, slowly, as though he didn't know what to do with them. He rested them on her shoulders.

But the touch seemed to loosen something inside him. Or maybe words were spoken between them, though the woman kept her grip tight around his waist. His hands moved around her, wrapping her in a true hug. Clinging to her as she did him.

Tears burned Elise's eyes, and she let them fall. He'd been

afraid of the reception he'd receive. Afraid of what his leaving would have done, both to the relationship and to his mother physically. At least one thing looked to be in fine shape. How could a mother not be overjoyed when her lost son returned to her?

Behind them, a man stepped forward. He was probably about the same age as the woman, though he didn't look like the years had aged him quite as much. He approached slowly, like he didn't want to interrupt. The emotion on his face was hard to gauge. Was he still angry with his son? His expression didn't look like joy exactly.

Goes Ahead must have caught sight of him, for he straightened, then pulled one of his hands from his mother's back so she could move beside him. He still kept one arm tight around her.

The sound of voices carried over the distance, but not loud enough to make out words even if Elise could understand the language. The woman exclaimed something to the man first, and her excitement was evident in her tone. Then the older fellow spoke to Goes Ahead, his voice much more controlled. Goes Ahead's strong baritone responded. Oh, if Elise could only know what they were saying.

Then Goes Ahead turned, the woman moving with him. His gaze landed on Elise and hovered there. She gave him an encouraging smile, though he might not have caught the full effect of it over the distance.

He spoke, then released his mother and started a quick stride toward Elise. When he reached her, his gaze searched out hers. "My mother and father. I want you and the little ones to meet them." His eyes said so much more. He was still worried. No longer concerned about whether his parents still lived, but worried about how they would accept these new people who were so important to him. Maybe there was something else, but no matter what, she and Goes Ahead would face it together.

She gave another encouraging smile. "Do you want to carry Walking Bird?"

He scooped his son from the horse's back, slipping a hand under the wounded leg in the way that had proved to be most comfortable for the lad. As Walking Bird locked his arms around his father's neck, Goes Ahead murmured, "We're going to meet your *nabésiibh* and *níiibh*. They are very happy to meet you." He spoke English, and a fresh wave of love washed through her.

She was already starting to learn Atsina, a language surprisingly easier for her to remember than any of the other tribal tongues she'd attempted so far. Or maybe it was the way Goes Ahead taught her—a kiss was an excellent reward for remembering yesterday's lesson. But he always used English when he spoke with his children to include her in conversations.

His gaze catching Elise's, he nodded for her to walk with him. She glanced back to make sure Ben and the others would be fine with the horses. Or maybe she looked to make sure her brother didn't appear disgruntled or concerned about her stepping away from him.

She shouldn't have worried.

Ben stood with the stallion's rope in one hand, the reins for their two mounts in his other, and a grin spreading across his face. He and Goes Ahead and White Owl had enjoyed many a conversation over dinner around the campfire these last few weeks, telling stories about other journeys through the mountains, funny tales about horses who had been fun to ride and some who hadn't been quite as pleasant, and a host of other life experiences. The bonding of brothers was well on its way.

She turned back to the village and the aged couple hobbling forward. The man had taken the woman's arm as they progressed together.

Elise and Goes Ahead met them in the open area, and as they stopped three steps apart, a myriad of emotions poured over his mother's face. Her focus had flicked to Elise a couple times, but for the most part, her eyes drank in Walking Bird. The sling hid Pretty Shield's sleeping face, so Elise turned for them to see her also.

The older woman's gaze grew wide as she caught sight of the babe, and she pressed fingers to her mouth. Her other trembling hand raised toward them, and a sheen welled in her eyes. The man shifted closer to her, still gripping her arm as though he thought she might swoon.

Goes Ahead spoke in Atsina, motioning to Walking Bird. The boy straightened as his grandmother smiled a wide grin through her tears. She responded in the same tongue, speaking to Walking Bird. Whatever she said pulled a shy smile from the boy.

Then Goes Ahead stepped closer to Elise and placed one hand at her back as he used the other to pull aside the sling even more to better show his daughter. His side pressed against Elise's, and she relished his warm strength next to her.

His mother had both hands pressed to her mouth now, awe lighting her features as she took a small step forward. He spoke again, probably telling her she could touch the babe, for his mother glanced at him, then closed the last of the distance. Her gaze lifted and met Elise's eyes for a suspended minute, and a kind of knowing smile lit the woman's face. There was acceptance there, buried somewhere in her overwhelming joy at meeting these precious grandchildren.

When she dipped her gaze to Pretty Shield and began murmuring to the babe, Elise glanced at Goes Ahead.

He faced his father, and the two of them were speaking quietly. It was hard to tell what the man thought about this homecoming.

But as Goes Ahead patiently responded to each comment or question, his father's bearing seemed to ease, little by little. His mouth even tipped up on one side in the hint of a smile. Then as he spoke, he looked to Elise, though he must still be speaking to Goes Ahead.

Goes Ahead turned to her too and switched to English. "My father wishes to know who this lovely woman is who holds my daughter as though she is her own."

She grinned, doing her best to hold in the flurry of nerves that erupted in her middle.

He turned back, looked from his father to his mother, and spoke in a tone of introduction as he switched to Atsina. As he spoke, his father nodded and his mother lifted her gaze to Elise.

Goes Ahead changed to English again. "Elise, this is my father, He Who Speaks Loud, and my mother, Straight Arm."

She smiled at his father first, then the woman standing just in front of her. Straight Arm's grin seemed to stretch even wider, and her hand moved as though she wanted to touch Elise's face. Instead, she turned to her son and stretched up toward his face, but she couldn't reach him until he lowered his head. She pressed a hand over each of his ears to pull him closer, then she touched a weathered kiss to one cheek, then the other.

The act held so much love, Elise's chest ached.

When his mother finally pulled back, Goes Ahead straightened. He wrapped his arm around Elise's waist to pull her closer, and she tucked herself in. Standing at Goes Ahead's side, with Pretty Shield in her arms and Walking Bird grinning at her, the moment felt more right than any she'd ever experienced.

With God's help, she'd have a lifetime of moments just like this.

Did you enjoy Goes Ahead and Elise's story? I hope so!
Would you take a quick minute to leave a review where you purchased the book?
It doesn't have to be long. Just a sentence or two telling what you liked about the story!

To receive a free book and get updates when new Misty M. Beller books release, go to https://mistymbeller.com/freebook

And here's a peek at the next book in the series, *Joy on the Mountain Peak* (Ben's story):

CHAPTER ONE

SPRING, 1833

NEAR THE MARIAS RIVER, FUTURE MONTANA TERRITORY

"He needs one more rock on his head. A big one."

Ben Lane pressed against the boulder hiding him from the women's voices as he replayed the words in his mind. Something rang familiar in that hushed tone, like the aroma of a favorite dessert he hadn't eaten in years. As it happened, he hadn't eaten *any* of his favorite foods in years. Two full years, in fact, since he and his sister left Illinois to go west and become missionaries to the Indian tribes.

And that's about how long it had been since he'd heard that same half-whisper, half-frantic tone.

Yet it couldn't be.

The sounds of stones clanking against each other drew his focus back to what might be happening on the other side of his hiding spot. Surely they weren't striking a man on the head with a rock.

He shifted sideways to peer around the boulder. Two figures worked over a cluster of rocks. Both wore long skirts, not the knee length buckskin that clad the women in the Gros Ventre village.

White women.

His mind stuttered to catch up with what he was seeing. It wasn't like he'd not seen white women in so long. His sister was with him, after all. And Lola, who'd been working with her Shoshone husband as a translator for them this past year. But both Elise and Lola had taken to wearing buckskins through the winter as their fabric skirts wore out. Leather kept the women much warmer through these long frigid months. Far more practical, and the two ladies didn't stand out as much from the people they were living and working among.

Which made these two individuals he'd stumbled upon stand out all the more. They looked like they'd just stepped through the doors of a shop on Main Street back home in Marcyville. What were they doing in this wilderness, at least two months' journey from any form of civilization?

One of the women turned away from the pile of rocks but stayed partly bent as she scanned the ground.

From this new angle, a jolt of recognition swept through him. It couldn't be. How could…?

His mind stuttered to a slow crawl even as an ache pressed in his chest—pain he'd worked hard to push aside these past two years. One glimpse of her brought all the anguish crashing over him like an avalanche.

Her gaze raked the grass around her, then lifted to the hedge of stones and brush that blocked her position from view on three sides. Before he could duck away, her eyes snagged on his.

He froze—a rabbit confronted by a fox. Yet she was no fox,

as much as the sight of her made his throat clog and a spurt of panic jolt through him.

How had Heidi found him out here?

~

Heidi Wallace straightened as her pulse thundered through her neck.

Those eyes. When she'd first caught sight of him, she thought natives were attacking. But her heart needed only a single beat before she recognized that intense gaze. The brown eyes she'd seen in her dreams so many nights since he'd left.

As Benjamin Lane slowly stepped from behind the boulder, she straightened to her full height and squared her shoulders. Part of her had known there was a chance she might run into him if she went west with Philip, no matter how vast this country stretched. It seemed fate thought it funny to toss the two of them together once more. Or maybe she and Ben really were intended for each other, no matter how much of a rapscallion he'd been back in Marcyville. A tiny part of her heart tried to lift at that idea, but she pressed it down. She'd spent far too long working to get over this man to ever allow him space in that particular organ again.

But it was good they'd met now. At last, she could finally get answers.

Benjamin stood there, watching her. His eyes proved impossible to read, as though the beard that now covered his face also shielded his expressions. The scruff made him look almost like one of the mountain men they'd met along the journey up the Missouri River, especially with the leather clothing he wore. But this was just a costume, a slight shift of appearance that covered the Benjamin she'd known for so long.

Loved for so long.

"Who is it, Heidi?" Temperance's low question broke through her thoughts and drew Ben's attention to her friend too.

Heidi shifted so she could see them both, then lifted a hand to motion toward each as she made formal introductions. "Miss Temperance McDonough, may I present Mr. Benjamin Lane." She raised her brows at Ben. "Or should I say Reverend Lane now?"

A flush pinkened his ears. At least, hopefully he had the good sense to be embarrassed, though it could just be sunburn from living outside all the time.

He shook his head as his eyes turned earnest. "I'm no minister. Just a man working to tell a lot of nice people about the God who loves them."

Tenderness pecked at her resolve. That was the Benjamin she'd known, the man who simply wanted to help others, whether it be a study session to aid the new girl in catching up at school or inviting that same lonely young woman home for Sunday lunch with his family so she would feel like she belonged.

But she couldn't let him crash through her defenses so easily. He'd not injure her again. She'd learned her lesson well.

Standing a little straighter, she nodded, then finished the introductions. "Mr. Lane then. Miss McDonough is my maid, assisting me on the journey."

A glance at Temperance showed her friend watched Heidi with one auburn brow raised. She must have picked up on the fact that Heidi had introduced Ben to her, not the other way around. In polite society, that would mean Temperance held the higher position, which would be a set-down to Ben. Perhaps he'd not picked up on the detail, but Temperance certainly had. Heidi let the corner of her mouth twitch so Temperance would know she'd done it on purpose.

When Heidi turned her attention back to Ben, he was eyeing the mound of rocks behind her. A fresh wave of emotion swept through her. Panic, but definitely laced with sadness. Poor Philip. Not even a man as frustrating as he was should have suffered so much in his last hours.

How should she explain the situation to Benjamin if he asked? Would he realize those stones covered a grave?

The lines at his eyes had tightened. The knot at his throat worked as he swallowed. Then he nodded toward the rocks. "Is there someone buried under there?"

He didn't shift his focus to her, just kept his gaze locked on that mound. At least that allowed her to breathe while she scrambled for an explanation that wouldn't reveal everything.

But Temperance's voice broke the silence instead. "Why that's her husband, sir. Mr. Philip."

Heidi locked her jaw to keep from wilting with dismay. That was the line they'd all agreed to give, but...not to *Benjamin Lane*.

Ben's eyes widened as they shifted to her, and the incredulity there almost covered the hurt that glimmered beneath.

Oh, if only she could melt into the ground like snow in summer. She forced herself to hold his gaze. To keep her chin high.

She might have some explaining to do, but so did he.

Get JOY ON THE MOUNTAIN PEAK at your favorite retailer!

ALSO BY MISTY M. BELLER

Call of the Rockies

Freedom in the Mountain Wind

Hope in the Mountain River

Light in the Mountain Sky

Courage in the Mountain Wilderness

Faith in the Mountain Valley

Honor in the Mountain Refuge

Peace in the Mountain Haven

Grace on the Mountain Trail

Calm in the Mountain Storm

Joy on the Mountain Peak

Brides of Laurent

A Warrior's Heart

A Healer's Promise

A Daughter's Courage

Hearts of Montana

Hope's Highest Mountain

Love's Mountain Quest

Faith's Mountain Home

Texas Rancher Trilogy

The Rancher Takes a Cook

The Ranger Takes a Bride

The Rancher Takes a Cowgirl

Wyoming Mountain Tales

A Pony Express Romance

A Rocky Mountain Romance

A Sweetwater River Romance

A Mountain Christmas Romance

The Mountain Series

The Lady and the Mountain Man

The Lady and the Mountain Doctor

The Lady and the Mountain Fire

The Lady and the Mountain Promise

The Lady and the Mountain Call

This Treacherous Journey

This Wilderness Journey

This Freedom Journey (novella)

This Courageous Journey

This Homeward Journey

This Daring Journey

This Healing Journey

ABOUT THE AUTHOR

Misty M. Beller is a *USA Today* bestselling author of romantic mountain stories, set on the 1800s frontier and woven with the truth of God's love.

Raised on a farm and surrounded by family, Misty developed her love for horses, history, and adventure. These days, her husband and children provide fresh adventure every day, keeping her both grounded and crazy.

Misty's passion is to create inspiring Christian fiction infused with the grandeur of the mountains, writing historical romance that displays God's abundant love through the twists and turns in the lives of her characters.

Sharing her stories with readers is a dream come true for Misty. She writes from her country home in South Carolina and escapes to the mountains any chance she gets.

Connect with Misty at www.MistyMBeller.com

Made in the USA
Monee, IL
10 September 2022

13667443R00121